I0580904

Carquinez Review

2024

ISBN 978-1-7354999-4-9
Library of Congress Control Number: 2024935310

Published by Benicia Literary Arts
P.O. Box 1903
Benicia, California 94510
www.benicialiteraryarts.org

Benicia Literary Arts, founded in 2012, encourages reading and writing in the community by producing events, creating a community of writers and readers, encouraging their development, and publishing their works of poetry, fiction, and non-fiction.

BLA Board President and Project Editor: Lois Requist
BLA Editor-in-Chief: Mary Eichbauer
Editorial Committee: Mary Eichbauer, Lois Requist, Ken Weichel
Book design by Jan Malin of Canyon Rose Press
Art selection: Jean Parnell and Celeste Smeland of Arts Benicia

Special thanks to: Linda Collins, Lois Kazakoff, Kristine Meitzner, Sherry Sheehan, Bob Stanley, Gayle Vassar, Lisa Wrenn.

Cover art: Steve Barbaria, *Still. Life. Ukraine, Winter 2023* (oil and acrylic on wood panel, 2023)

Introduction

The Benicia Literary Arts Board of Directors is proud to present to you this third volume of Carquinez Review. Benicia is known as a hotbed for the arts. Visual artists, prose writers, and poets live and practice their work in this small, historic town on the Carquinez Strait. This third volume is bursting with examples of the kind of work that is being created here today. In these pages, you'll find poetry in many forms, prose that ranges from true stories to flights of fancy, and artworks in several media: painting, drawing, collage, photography.

The work for this anthology originated with an open call for materials. Writing received by the deadline was stripped of anything identifying the authors and then evaluated anonymously by four prose judges and two poetry judges, according to a predetermined rating system. Arts Benicia carried out a similar process to select the visual artworks. We feel confident that the final product represents a cross-section of art and writing from communities located around the Carquinez Strait, from Benicia and Vallejo to Fairfield, Walnut Creek, Martinez, Pittsburg, Oakland, El Sobrante, and other Bay Area and Central Valley communities.

As with any collection of work, this one can be read, or browsed, in any order. Page through and glance at the artwork, reading a poem or a short prose piece as you pass by. Later, settle down with one of the longer prose works and a cup of coffee or tea. One word of advice: don't miss any of these varied works. Each has something different and valuable to offer.

Lois Requist, Board President
Mary Eichbauer, Editor-in-Chief

(Previous editions of Carquinez Review came out in 2000 and 2020 and are still available at *www.benicialiteraryarts.org.*)

Art Collectors by Diana Krevsky, paint and collage writings over architectural layout, 2013

Contents

V. Arrivals

VI. In the Dying Season

VII. Character Tales

Artwork

Eckley Pier finds a steamboat past by Lori Larks, acrylic on
Ampersand Gessoboard, 2023

I. Art and Beauty

A Bridge in the Fog
by Thomas Stanton

Sometimes practice paintings
Like practice songs
Become
The mythic one
Everything
Following a perfect painting
With things
Well-struck in
Bold and simple
With memories reduced filigree
Details suggestive, evidential
The beauty of this
Like beauty itself
Cannot be well-predicted
And all and every, that follows
Becomes
A copy
Some greater
Some not so much
Each iteration
A prayer
Some answered
Some not so much
The bridge of the painter
The bridge of the song
Often
Where the heart
Lies.

The Humming

by Thomas Stanton

I listen to you
With the cello just here
Close and near as can be

The cello keeping its secrets
Here's the decoding
The varnish

Though the cello
Not resonating
With rich familiar lyric

Usually the one
To have done
The writing
Upon the strings

Begins
To softly
Sing.

Pantoum for Mary's Hibiscus

by Deborah Bachels Schmidt

I was planted when the house was new,
a century ago, the China rose,
the tropical hibiscus, in harmony
with creamy stucco walls and red tile roof.

A century ago, the China rose...
I remember how I spread my branches
against the walls, below the red tile roof,
opening crimson blossoms to the sun.

I remember how when I spread my branches
my arms were filled with tiny singing birds.
I opened crimson blossoms in the sun
and let them fall uncounted on the path.

My arms were filled with tiny singing birds.
But years have passed me by, so many years
fallen like the flowers on the path.
It's whitefly, I'm afraid, the gardener said.

The years have passed her by, too many years.
All we can do is cut her down and hope,
he said. *The dreaded whitefly, I'm afraid.*
And so I have been cut down to my knees.

All we can do is cut her down and hope.
All through the winter you will fear I'm dead,
branchless, leafless, cut down to my knees.
But underneath the ground I'll stir and hum

all through the winter, though you fear I'm dead,
readying shoots to send up in the spring.
Beneath the ground I'll stir and dream of how
my arms will fill once more with singing birds.

Search and Rescue

Haiku Diary, Summer 2022

by Tamar Enoch

"Haiku is a personal history, and each one is composed to make a lifetime."—Takaha Shugyo *

Walnut Creek, California

For the last year and a half, I have been writing haiku several times a week. I compose at least half of them on my back porch, sipping my morning cup of green tea. I keep expecting to run out of things to say about the trees, hills and living creatures I can see from there, but it hasn't happened yet. The incongruous palm fronds just peeking over the top of a mature oak reminded me of a kid who poses for a picture holding two fingers behind his friend's head.

> *Mischievous fronds*
> *Wiggle over the tall oak's crown—*
> *California palm*

This next haiku is about the Hebrew conversation group I go to twice a month. I grew up speaking Hebrew, although I am ambivalent about Israel and my identity as a Jewish person. But speaking the language brings old memories back to life, like those rare fire poppies that bloom after forest fires. So, I agreed to join, but only after everyone in the group promised never to bring up politics.

> *Circle of women*
> *Speaking the language we lost*
> *Shaded by old trees*

A friend asked me to pet-sit her goldfish, and, to my surprise, I became quite fond of the little creature.

It's enough like love.
The way my goldfish flutters
When I pass her bowl

On May 25, 2022, I woke to the news of the horrible school shooting in Uvalde. Nineteen children and two adults killed by a deranged teenager with an assault rifle. Yearning to create some sense of normalcy on a day when it seemed nothing would ever make sense again, I decided to go for a swim. At the pool, the person in the next lane complained that I was splashing her as I swam. She was in a pool and expected everyone to make sure she stayed dry? But it would only make things worse to direct snide remarks at her. I should have just moved over a few lanes. On that day of all days, couldn't we live in harmony?

There's a small ornamental pond on my way home from the pool. I have driven past hundreds of times, but after the swimming pool fracas, on an impulse, I stopped to explore it. Under a birch tree decked with streamers of fresh green leaves, I closed my eyes and let the sound of flowing water wash through me.

Midair liaison
Scarlet dragonflies couple
In the pond's green light

A few days later, I was in the Oakland Airport, beginning a trip to visit family in Kansas and North Carolina. A judge had just struck down the CDC's mask mandate for interstate travel, so even though COVID cases were skyrocketing across the country, only a few people were wearing masks. As I waited for the call to board my flight, a young family strolled by—father, toddler, mother carrying an infant—all unmasked. Last summer, a friend's infant grandson fell gravely ill with COVID. And now, overnight, taking reasonable precautions to stop the spread of a serious disease had become passé.

> *Unmasked travelers*
> *Reveal more than their faces*
> *By the airport gate*

Lawrence, Kansas

Lawrence, Kansas, where my 88-year-old mother lives, was my first stop of the journey. That morning, I woke to a classic midwestern thunderstorm.

> *Patiently, the earth*
> *Endures mysterious rage*
> *Summer thunderstorm*

I am exposed to fresh outpourings of anger every day, even if all I do is open my email. Maybe we are all in the middle of some kind of collective temper tantrum.

While in Lawrence, I continued the slow, difficult work of going through the old boxes of letters and mementoes that were put in storage when my mother moved out of her home almost ten years ago now. This time, it was a box of letters my great aunt and uncle had received in the 1930s and 40s. My aunt had left her home and family in Wisconsin to work in New

York City, a level of independence that was very unusual for young women at that time. Her fiancé, my uncle, was signalman on a Navy destroyer. From the letters, I gathered that his enlistment had shocked his family. As a 30-year-old attorney, he could have either stayed at his safe desk job, or applied for an office job with the Navy.

I read about a dozen letters, extracting them from their brittle envelopes, unfolding them for the first time in fifty years. They reported the day-to-day minutiae of these long-ago lives—movies, birthday parties, minor illnesses, along with speculation about the war and when it was ever going to end—little details affirming the connection between people living far from each other, in the days before long-distance phone calls, let alone emails and texts.

As I read, I began to sense the permission of these long-gone people, most of whom I had never met, to let go of these communiqués. I guess even they didn't want their sniffles and quarrels to outlive them.

The gaping dumpster—
I surrender old letters
Freeing ancient ghosts

Emerald Isle, North Carolina

From Kansas, I continued on to North Carolina for a beach vacation my sister and I had been planning since she visited me in California last summer. The Carolina beach is very different from the rocky, frigid seashore of California. The ocean is warm and velvety, the sand is smooth and yielding.

Lost in the word "blue,"
A roiled ocean reflecting
Gradations of sky

Being at the Carolina beach brought back so many memories. Although I hadn't been there for over a decade, there was a time when we had family reunions there every year. The first time we went, my sister was pregnant with her son, Noah, who is now 31 years old. I was visiting from England, where I was doing a post-doctoral fellowship. A year later, I would move to Boston, and, for the next ten years, I would spend at least one weekend on the beach each year. My parents would be there too—my father, vigorous and healthy before his disabling stroke; my driven, opinionated mother taking a rare break from her myriad meetings and emails; my sister's former husband, a saxophone player who taught Noah to boogie board and shared a passion for windsurfing with my father.

Returning again—
Old dreams and ghosts mingling
Under a broad sky

As the days went by, I found myself going back even further, reliving my own childhood memories of beach vacations.

Frolicking ocean
The ever-willing companion
of childhood summers

I am sky walking
On a thin film of water
Between sea and land

My father is dead, my mother incapacitated by dementia. My sister has been divorced for more than 15 years. Noah, the round-faced little boy with a shy, sweet smile, has become a tall muscular man who builds trails for the Forest Service. And I am in my sixties, recently retired, starting to understand that there is less of life in front of me than behind me.

The receding tide—
Each wave giving up the shore
Just a bit sooner

One evening, my sister insisted on watching the January 6th Commission hearings on television. We hadn't listened to the news all week and I didn't want to puncture my temporary bubble of blissful ignorance. I sat out on the porch instead, watching a storm roll by, trying my best to ignore the murmurings from the television.

Insurrection hearings—
Outside, the silent flashes
Of distant lightning

Each morning I went for a barefoot walk along the beach. I was intrigued by the banks of clams, revealed for a moment each time the waves swept away a layer of sand.

Low tide uncovers
This teeming metropolis
Of burrowing clams

There are so many things we don't know or see, some of them happening right beneath our feet.

Form or Freedom?

When I write, a phrase or a sentence about something I see comes to me and I build a haiku out from that. On our last morning on the beach, something struck me about the sight of our swimming suits, pegged to the clothesline. The three lines of this haiku all came to me at the same time.

Hung out to dry
Our empty swimming suits
Dance without us

It has been my practice to follow the traditional Japanese 17-syllable haiku form: 5 in the first line, 7 in the second, 5 in the last. Some poets are adamant that English haiku should follow these rules. There are gifted poets who argue just as forcefully for a freer form, but I have always tried to be faithful to the 5–7–5 form. Since my haiku had only 14 syllables, I chewed on my pen until I could see a way to insert 3 more syllables.

Hung out on the line
Our empty swimming suits sway
Dancing without us

I posted both haiku to a Facebook haiku group, asking my readers to tell me which poem they liked better. The post was much more popular than my posts usually are—I got 108 reactions and more than 40 comments. By a small margin, 16 to 14, my readers who expressed a preference chose the free-form haiku. There were also about eight readers who said they liked both, and then a few who took it upon themselves to scramble my words into what they considered to be an improved version of the haiku.

After I got home, I revised the haiku again, sticking with 5–7–5.

Last day on the beach
Our drying swimming suits sway
Dancing without us

"Last day on the beach" links the image of the swimming suits to the feeling of the end of a beach vacation. For a brief period, the place seemed to belong to us, and as we prepared to leave, we gave up that illusion, leaving "our" beach to the next set of vacationers. Given our ages and life's uncertainties, who knew if we would ever return?

There's a romantic notion that haiku should be completely spontaneous, like a Zen Master's shout. But, in my experience, a frank response to a moment is only part of what makes a haiku that satisfies. Other ingredients are time, distance and patience. The Zen Master's shout takes years of practice. And you don't know what works and what doesn't unless you have readers to tell you.

Hillsborough, North Carolina

I spent my last night in North Carolina at my sister's house. We were tired after the long drive back from the beach. We unpacked, ate dinner, then settled on her screened-in porch with a cup of herbal tea (me) and a glass of wine (my sister). She lit the candle seated in an ornate wrought-iron mobile hanging from a hook in the ceiling. A parent of one of her piano students had given it to her as barter for a semester of lessons. As night fell, a pattern of geometric shadows began to dance on the walls and floor.

> *On the porch at dusk*
> *How the candle-cast shadows*
> *Sharpen into stars*

My sister and I are very different, and we often misunderstand each other, but she's also my oldest friend. It felt good to sit together in silence as the night came on.

Search and Rescue

The next morning, my departure day, we got up early. Since it was going to be hot, my sister decided we ought to take her dog for an early morning walk. We left through her back gate, stopping to chat with a neighbor. Without warning, his dog, a young, wiry pit bull-boxer mix, bounded off his porch and attacked my sister's dog, a frail, aging beagle-ish rescue she's had for 14 years. I spent the rest of the morning accompanying them to urgent care appointments.

A piece of the dog's ear was missing, and my sister was also injured—her own dog bit her hand as she tried to protect him from the attacker. Fortunately, they are both expected to recover completely, especially critical for my sister, who makes her living teaching and playing the piano. Still for days after my return, images of the brawl kept flashing before my eyes. I had to stop, breathe, and bring myself back into the present, reminding myself it was over and we were all going to be okay.

I wasn't sure how, or even if, I should write a haiku about this incident. Classical haiku are about the beauties of nature and usually include one of around 500 agreed-upon "season words" (kigo) such as "willow," "cherry blossoms," or "harvest moon." "Pit bull" is not on any list of haiku season words. That didn't stop me from trying, but, despite numerous drafts, I could not write a haiku that worked.

At last it occurred to me to write instead about dandelions, a venerable and traditional haiku subject. I had written several dandelion haiku earlier in the year for a contest, and perhaps that prepared the ground for this poem's emergence.

Certainties scattered
In just the space of a breath—
Dandelion puff

I grieve, not only for my sister's pain, but also for the way the shock of the attack now overshadows the precious week of beach time we spent together for the first time in so many years. Collating these haiku is my search and rescue operation. I want to excavate these moments from the rubble, hoping that one day they will shine again.

Maybe I also long to leave a message to the citizens of some more peaceful time in humanity's future. If they exist, they will know all about the sickness, the violence, the looming ecological disasters of our era. But let them also know we had dragonflies and goldfish, that we counted haiku syllables, that we walked by the ocean with the people we loved.

> *A world demolished*
> *A thousand set in motion*
> *Dandelion puff*

* *The Earth Afloat: Anthology of Contemporary Japanese Haiku,* Kato, K. and Burleigh, D. eds.

Sinister Symphonic Haunting!

by Alyza Lee Salomon

Ever since the brazen night-after-
Halloween concert, I can't
get *Rhapsody in Blue*
out of my mind—
                no matter
what else I listen to.
A little Telemann piece
on KDFC last night
didn't scare away the
                    percussion
and the lilting syncopation
dancing through my brain.
Only problem is
my mental orchestra
                  is nowhere
near as good
as the real McCoy—Oy!
What to do? Maybe
some Rimsky-Korsakov,
                  a little
Ralph Vaughan Williams,
some Pachelbel, Mozart, or Chopin,
and finally, if all else fails,
give me *Afternoon of a Faun*—
                    Yes!
Debussy, do the job, play me
the ultimate, magical cure!
This quicksilver sun-dappled spell
ought to clear my beleaguered head
                    —for sure!

Benicia Sunset by Annette Laurel Batchelor, oil, 2021

What Is a Poem?

by Louise Moises

A poem doesn't care
if last night the garbage disposal stopped working,
and when I opened the refrigerator, the light was out.
A poem doesn't care
that it wasn't the garbage disposal or the fridge,
but the circuit box.
How at 9 PM I put on my robe and slippers,
and with my flashlight, tried to be Wonder Woman,
and failed.
A poem doesn't care that I failed,
frustrated by my inability to solve the problem,
the need to call a handyman,
when I really longed to be self-sufficient.
A poem is not my frustration or the handyman.
But maybe I'm wrong. Perhaps a poem
should be the handyman, who generously calls me back
and shows up this morning just as promised,
although he is unable to solve the problem.
Maybe poems are the ordinary people
who passed through our lives,
the friend that calls every day to make sure
I'm still okay,
the neighbor who asks if there's anything I need.
Perhaps a poem is the fear I feel
over the state of our country;
how do I turn off the news, block my ears,
because I don't want to hear any more.

Maybe a poem is silence
that allows me to hear my breath,
or how my hands look like my mother's.
The older I get, the more I resemble her.
Yes, that's it. A poem is my face in the mirror,
growing older without any means of halting time,
accepting the face and the mirror,
that is the poem.

Footsteps by Ken Weichel, collage, 1980

II. The Well of Memory

Anemoia

by Evie Groch

I wander through the confined cottage
in silent shoes.
It's bathed in dim light that sneaks
beyond clouded windowpanes,
paints stone walls in grey despair,
imbues me with a melancholy mood
of metaphoric longing.

Rough-hewn oak shelves support
lengthy-titled tomes of tortured history,
tarnished and bruised bronze candlesticks,
wood-framed photos of family
members long gone.

The soot-lined hearth emits little heat
from the heaps of nostalgia on the grate.
The interior uncluttered, yet haphazardly
strewn with random piles of yarn,
unfinished knitting projects, failed attempts
at elegantly styled letters scattered
on the writing desk around an ink well.

A birch cradle rocks itself without a breeze;
a rocking chair shares the movement.
Flimsy gingham curtains sway with
little encouragement. Vintage bottles
stand like retired soldiers, ready once
more to fulfill onerous orders.

Devoid of people, quiet with tranquility,
familiar feelings fill me in strange ways.
Is this loneliness, regret, an imagined
scene in my unconscious? An untriggered
false memory or simply anemoia,
my nostalgic sense of longing for a past
I never lived from an era I wasn't born in?

A Moment in Time

by Evie Groch

Time paints the past
in sepia tones,
softens the focus
with blurred boundaries,
captures a moment
we didn't know would matter.

A hem unraveling, a smudge
on her face, a bee set to sting,
a ladder before its fall,
the clear day before the storm,
laundry hangs like sails
in place atop an ill wind.

Posts in the countryside,
frills in the city,
empty roads leading nowhere,
history sits still.

Moments amass, sort themselves
into a catalogued tome
with a leather-bound, titled spine,
one who slides into its proper decade.

Bless This Food

by Linda Hastings

Whe n we first met, any meals we shared were serious business meetings with stressful agendas and stiff negotiations. My West Coast company hired his East Coast company to complete a seventy-million-dollar building project. He was the vendor; I was the client project manager. I knew people; he knew numbers. He was the expert; I held the authority. We needed each other. So much pressure. It felt like a haphazard, wet and wild, white-water rafting trip that went on 24/7—hearts pounding, potential death by drowning, risk of wrapping a rock any minute, yet great adventure.

These were 14-hour days, nights of fitful sleep, day-old donuts, cold coffee and lunchroom pizza. My office was stuffed with stacks of blueprints, design samples, schematics, and spreadsheets. The required decisions were overwhelming, and the buck stopped with me. Priorities kept shifting; everything felt like life or death. No time for wine or wishful thinking.

Finally, after five intense years of overcoming the inevitable construction delays and budget overruns, the work was finished. I had learned about change orders, endangered bird species, and earthquake codes. He had learned about human dynamics and the importance of communication and consensus. We had learned we could trust each other. The tall, shimmering blue-glass building at the end of a winding road on a hill was stunning. The grand opening was a county-wide celebration with dignitaries and politicians in attendance. Three hundred staff moved into the beautiful space. But we couldn't let go; our story was just beginning.

Soon we were meeting up for romantic rendezvous in the City of San Francisco. Since he was so gallant in his courting and this was not his hometown, where we ate was my choice. Looking back, I was clueless. Here was this Southern engineer, a seemingly old-fashioned, shy, refined man with substantial means. Yet, I decided to take him to all the newest "happening" places in town. He was patient and sparkly eyed as we waited, standing, in noisy, crowded, hip restaurants where reservations were grudgingly accommodated. He managed to look calm and uncomfortable in his shiny, stiff leather oxfords, his buttoned-up Brooks Brothers suit jacket and perfectly knotted silk tie, his hands clasped loosely in front of him.

Every two to three weeks he would fly in from Atlanta for a couple of days, rent a car and check into a hotel in Union Square. I would drive over from the suburbs to meet him. Each time we met, he reached for me with just his forearms and gentle hands extended in a narrow, awkward gesture. He was slow to allow full exposure of his heart space. The bold gaze of his dark brown eyes plunged into my light blue ones.

Later I understood the sweetness of both of our efforts. Me, anxious to please and impress, fluttering about with indecision—booking multiple dinner reservations, worrying what time was best, and then fretting about which one would feed his fancy. Him, just quietly adoring, waiting to eat, ready to pay the bill, and eager to get back to just the two of us. Experienced gastrophiles, we relished the food along with the possibilities of it all. He said he loved to eat everything; he said there was nothing he didn't like. Later I discovered that was a bit of a stretch.

Within a year, I left my job, my friends, and my life on the coast of California. I hired a moving truck, rented out my house and boarded a plane to join him in Georgia, where his national company was headquartered. Soon we were living together in his Southern world and dealing with the day to day—working, shopping, cooking, laundry. We made a cozy and delicious home—we made a life.

We learned new pieces of each other. He wanted a place in the kitchen, who knew? My gourmet sauces were not his preference. His red meat was not mine. We ate our unbiased vegetables like good soldiers, for health, for strength. I preferred meals mid evening; his preference was before dark. We compromised easily on everything. When the dark swell of disagreement threatened to come between us, we stopped, faced each other, and said in tandem—"it doesn't matter"—a benefit, perhaps, of midlife. He washed, I cooked. He cooked, I washed. He pounded the meat, shucked the corn and managed the grill. I sautéed and seasoned and set the table. He delighted in lighting candles each night. One afternoon after work, he surprised me with a fluffy, white faux-fur rug that we spread in front of the fireplace or on the deck among the trees. Sometimes we picnicked in those places, naked. We fell into our very own effortless rhythm with a synchronicity that left us breathless.

Although there were cupids in our kitchen, there were also rules. Did you know that green beans don't go with steak? Green beans go with chicken. Asparagus goes with steak. Broccoli is equal opportunity. Salad dressing must always be on the side. Coconut in any form is taboo. Avocados are out. Capers must always be fried before using. Al dente is the mandatory method for all pasta, no exceptions. There would be no whole wheat or seeded bread consumed at our table—his homemade biscuits were the only way to go. Our brunches and dinners were achievements in harmony, every part coming together perfectly, better than a poem or a puzzle. A friend mentioned repeatedly that she loved to watch our "kitchen dance" as we made a meal, always tender and in step.

If I close my eyes, I can still feel the awe and gratitude of sitting down to a beautifully set table on an easy Sunday morning in front of a warm plate cradling his perfectly poached eggs on buttered crumpets, covered with my lemony smooth hollandaise and sides of crispy potatoes. Maybe a glass of champagne for me, sparkling water for him. Our "Mendocino music" would be playing on the stereo, the Sunday paper waiting, sun streaming through the skylights. A little cocoon of heaven was ours for those morning moments, suspended in temporary time while the wind rustled among the trees outside our windows.

I was a West Coast girl with a Bay Area fear of gravy, carbohydrates, and butter. My experience in preparing the voluptuous dishes of the South and of his Midwestern roots was limited. I did eventually learn that moderation really was the key, that I wouldn't actually die from macaroni and cheese, and that it could make me smile. He took over hash brown duty; mine were floppy and impatient and never cooked enough. When the holidays came, we agreed that my electric mixer mashed potatoes didn't cut it—they were too soupy and lumpy at the same time. They needed the traditional hand mash and stiff, forceful treatment—he was an expert. My gravy attempts turned into failed science projects: unnecessarily complex. He smiled and hugged me each time as he took the whisk from my hands and made gravy magic. So, these, among others, became his signature tasks. It seemed he took on what his Russian mother had left him with: an instinct to overcome the scarcity and withholding of the past, a determination for something more. We must be fed. There must always be plenty, and it must be the best it can be.

There were surprises! He cherished my scallops even though they were covered in sherry sauce. I mastered his mother's *golumpkis* (Polish stuffed cabbage rolls), remembered from his childhood. My lamb shanks were the best. And together we duplicated the tricky spaghetti carbonara from a dining extravaganza in Bermuda. His grilled lobster tails and melt-in-your-mouth pork ribs were unsurpassed. My Grand Marnier soufflés were without competition. He charred my Sunday football hot dogs against his better judgment, learned to love mushrooms in omelets, realized he actually enjoyed Indian food, and often requested my Cajun barbecued shrimp. Friends begged for his decadent grilled-cheese sandwiches that made them moan with pleasure. Never mind that I broke the rules and added pickles to mine. We were wrapped up in each other like layers of phyllo dough covered in warm melted butter.

During our twelve short years together, we traveled frequently to foreign places. We researched restaurants, chose carefully, and continued the serious effort of eating well. His range of culinary experience allowed easy detection of any preparation errors. He was a harsh critic and quick in his judgment or praise. Sometimes, when asked how his meal was, he would respond "edible" with obvious disappointment. I came to understand that this simply meant "nothing special." His was a quest for the extraordinary when it came to food and to love.

Then, all too soon, the cancer diagnosis eight years before took us into that alternate universe of testing and treatment, of hope and despair and the interminable waiting. Now it was his last Thanksgiving, just four days before the disease finally severed our togetherness. Having lost his taste buds, and with his organs slowing down, he hadn't eaten more than a few bites in almost a week. What could be worse for someone who found so much pleasure in his palate? He became a man of few words. He realized that what he was able to say through sheer force of will made little sense. The required transitions from day to night and back again were exhausting. The inevitable bodily functions, almost too much to bear.

I was thinking, I'll just get a turkey breast and some prepared dishes from the market to serve for this holiday dinner. I knew he wouldn't be attempting more than a bite or two. We talked about it while I sat on his lap. Or rather, I asked a series of questions. He indicated "Bring it on!" with a wink. He made it clear he wanted the traditional menu—turkey, mashed potatoes, stuffing, gravy, peas, yeast rolls. I prepared my preferred dishes as well, the fresh cranberries he said he didn't like but had never tasted, the sweet potatoes with marshmallows that were superfluous for him. For the first time, I handled all the tasks in the now solitary kitchen. He watched from his recliner chair across the room with a slight smile on his face. I used the hand masher for the potatoes and simplified my gravy process. Somehow, I got the turkey carved, or chunked, or something. It all came together for a last attempt at compromise and harmony and abundance.

His reticent children and their families came to dinner, not quite sure what to expect. He smiled gently through the whole thing, ate a few bites sitting in his dining chair at the head of the table, and then returned to his recliner and closed his eyes. He must have known or trusted that I was okay. I had conquered the kitchen alone and so, of course, I could do the unfathomable, continue without him in this life in spite of his promises to love me forever and never leave me.

The very next morning, he was disoriented and couldn't get out of bed. The hospice nurse arrived and asked him his name, which he provided. He volunteered my name as his wife and held up his index and middle finger, wiggling them together as we did, a sign of our togetherness "forever." But when she asked him if he knew where he was, he said, "the hospital, of course, in room 103." The end came quickly after that.

Since then, his spirit is always by my side in the kitchen. I can still feel his purposeful effort in considering what I would prefer and his pleased contentment in the acceptance of our choices. He provided the container within which it was safe to be myself—an enormous, inexplicable gift I carry with me now. I miss his encouragement and unconditional affection. I miss his strength and humor. The ordinary will always be just "edible."

Now, making eggs Benedict alone is a poignant and comforting experience—I can do it by myself after all. I warm the plates and make sure the potatoes are extra crispy. It turns out, perfectly poached eggs are actually achievable by me. I use the hand masher for mashed potatoes. I've learned that gravy is gravy and not a gourmet sauce. Our mixture of tastes became sacred, representing our laughter and the entwinement of our hearts. We were able to let go of ourselves and almost become each other's shadow souls, if only for a moment in time. A secret space just for us. We had exquisite joy and exquisite pain. It was a wonderful illusion of perfection, however limited.

Now I eat more whole wheat, less red meat, and lots of gourmet sauces.

I am still here...in my future.

He is still my forever angel and dance partner.

Moment by moment in this life, we give thanks for food, for sustenance, for bounty.

And most of all, for the miracle of love.

Music Hill

My Father's Sky

>*by Ramona Lappier*

Over the slopes
of Music Hill,
my father's sky is
shooting stars
and satellites
and a waxing moon
that brightens
the eastern birches
and makes silhouettes
of the tall pines.

If only our time together
were even half as wide
as the universe sparkling
in my father's eyes,
iridescent blue
and deep and wise,
reflecting limericks
and lullabies
and happy tunes
and scenic drives
and hot fudge sundaes
on Sunday afternoons,

but too soon, too soon
I will have to fly.
Tomorrow... today...
too soon to say goodbye.

Sometime after midnight
beneath my father's sky,
at the foot of Music Hill
I break open. I weep. I cry.

Putting Wrinkles Back

by Jane Russell

Apply miracle creams,
  seek Botox treatments,
possibly a face lift too.
  Advertisements are so convincing.
Aging is not acceptable.
  Youth and beauty are in vogue.
Lines of time should be erased.
  Beneath my aging face,
my self-image, a younger woman.
  Spirit of youth is still with me,
although my body resists,
  the mirror reflects the truth.
My outer image, reflected back,
  lets me see what others see.
Who is that old lady in the mirror?

Wrinkles are a roadmap of my life,
  joys and sorrows etched in my face.
Lines deepen as I smile or laugh.
  I am wiser now, an elder, a crone,
a sage to be listened to, respected.
  Should my life be denied
and all that has been,
  all that has chiseled character in my face?

Can I see my beauty within,
  love the character without?
I shall let others see me as I am.
  Wrinkles are not flaws
to be hidden or taken away.
  They are beauty marks
of life well lived.
  Time to put the wrinkles back.

Published in *Vistas and Byways Review*, OLLI, S.F.
State University, Issue 16, Fall 2023

Note Card

by Louise Moises

An envelope falls through the mail-slot,
blows across the room, a card
from my friend, two thousand miles away.
We write regularly.
Sharp knife slits open the small white envelope,
an apricot-colored card with a fluffy cat.

I read the first three lines, try to make sense
of the words, crammed together to fit the limit
of the margins, cursive script, blue ink,
painted words wander in her familiar scrawl.

How can it be, my friend
of the curly brown hair,
sparkling eyes, slim fit body of a swimmer,
with a dog to walk, a garden to tend,
a house to care for, a husband to love...?

The tumor,
removed six months ago, has returned,
invades other organs.
My hand goes to my belly,
in my chest, an ache, a slight nausea.

Outside the sun battles the clouds,
light and shadow. Chill air sifts
through the cracks around the door.
Scent of coffee lingers in the kitchen,
reminds me of the lunches we shared
when she was my neighbor.

Tuesday her treatment resumes.
Chemo will tear apart her body,
radiation sap her strength.
        The final line of her note...
            I will do all this because I want to live.

On Passover and Easter Sunday

by Karen Marker

We've come with a guitar to visit and sing
because she can't walk down
the steep stairs into a world full
of cars on Berkeley Way. She lies

in a hospital bed in front of the living
room window surrounded by spring
flowers that grow wild outside. Behind
her closed purple lid, a tear. Eyes open,

close, open again. Her long thin fingers sway.
Light prints the walls, the shelves full of art
she's made—pit fired plates, Arabic, Hebrew
letters, blessing bowls. Her mouth is

round like the curve in the clay as words come out
with little breaths. She says she's been waiting
too long for death, now without hospice. But she loves
the songs she remembers. We sing *jingle jangle morning*

as she did fifty years ago with Morty. Then we sing
Dayanu from the Seder's Passover story. All the things
that would have been enough on the way to freedom.
It has been enough, an entire extra year of life already

since the doctor said she'd die, ten years since Morton's
been gone. Ten years, she says, is enough.
Too many miracles. It's enough.

Mary and Linda

by Linda Wright

Mary and Linda did everything together. White and Black girls. Best friends since third grade. They rode their bikes around their white neighborhood in Oakland, California, walked with their swirling hula hoops up and down the sidewalk, and roller-skated to the park.

They cared for their Barbies and other dolls, ran to the store, helped each other with chores. Linda helped Mary set the table and Mary swept Linda's floors.

The friends attended different schools until one day, in 1972, Linda's Mother said, "To the same junior high school with Mary you will go." Linda told Mary with eyes bright but missed Mary's soft, "Oh no."

The weeks went by and Linda got ready. The two walked together to junior high. But at the school gate, Mary ditched Linda to join her own race, leaving Linda terrified: walking through strange halls, figuring out the racial rules in the lunchroom, and managing public showers.

On that first day, Linda saw Mary, who saw Linda, and Mary turned and went another way. Each and every time.

Linda, confused and hurt, got the message. At school, she and Mary couldn't be friends. In the early 1970s, no whites and Blacks were seen together in Oakland public schools, ever. But Linda didn't know this fact. At her old parochial school, white, brown, and Black enjoyed each other.

At the end of school, Mary waited at the school gate. The two old friends walked home talking about their separate days but never why Mary felt it had to be that way. Mary did not say why she could not have a Black person as a friend at school among her white school friends.

Each day, Mary ditched Linda at the school gate and waited there for the walk home. Never did they talk about how Linda felt about their separate days. Linda wanted to yell and demand what was up with Mary running from her during the entire day. But Linda's mouth couldn't form the words. Mary, in one day, became one of those whom Linda wouldn't trust with her true feelings. She never said a word about Mary running away. At home, Linda disappeared into her room, where she did not ignore the pain ripping her stomach apart as she cried over the lost friendship and her inability to speak up.

Linda's mother knew something bad had happened, but she didn't know what. Linda couldn't say the words that took away her smile, leaving her in gloom. On Friday, her mother gave Linda a black mutt that Linda called "Bertha Butt," because the dog waddled when she walked and because Jimmy Castor Bunch's "Bertha Butt Boogie" was one of Linda's favorite songs.

On Saturday, Mary knocked on Linda's front door, hoping she would come out and play. But she found Linda not willing to ride a bike, roller skate, or help her with chores.

Instead, Bertha Butt was curled up next to Linda while Linda's head was inside a book—her new best friends that didn't make her hurt.

A Pail for Blackberries

by Evie Groch

In my backyard of stony carpet
protruding from brambled fingers
hang the blackberries moist and full.
I love the way they paint my tongue
and corners of my lips with streaks
of dark sweetness, fill my mouth with joy
and my pockets with stains.

I'm a three-year old alone, unheeded,
in a little village far away, gathering
berries brazenly to suck their juice.
My blueish-purple mouth reveals my tasting;
my pockets drip with juice.

No friends, no toys, just blackberries
to pick and taste and hold. They suffice.
I'm scolded for discoloring the floral
frontpiece that covers my white frock.

The next day out to pick some more,
I have a pail swinging from my hand.
After a warning and a washing,
my mother spared us both.

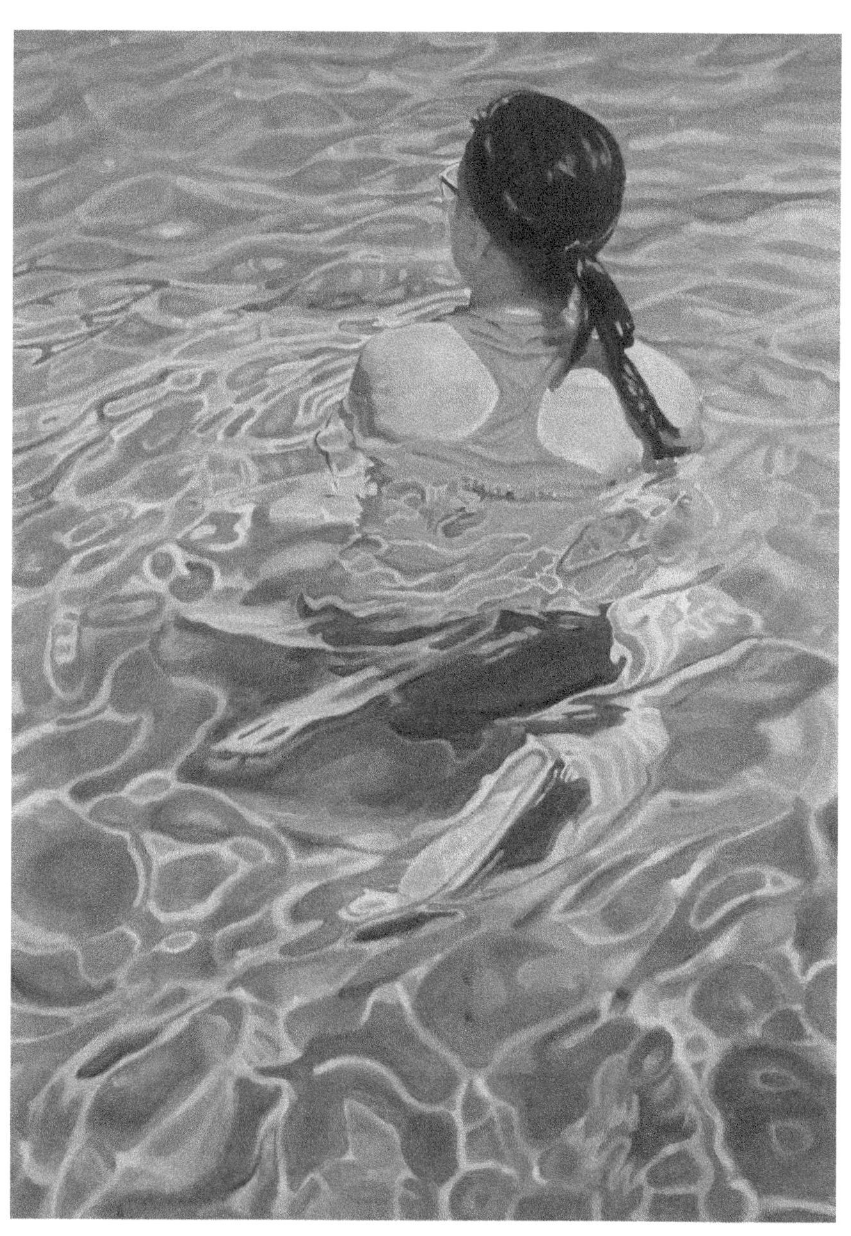

Shoreward Gaze by Claudia Waters, oil on linen, 2015

III. The Natural World

A River Washes Away

by Sandra Duncan Simmer

A river washes away tear drops
Fallen from the hearts of lonely trees
Collects the moss of ancient memories
From the underbellies of stones and rocks
Cleanses sins in its fast-paced flow

A river washes away lovers' kisses
Tossed carelessly from a country bridge
Mixes the essence of their passion
Into its frothy churning brew
Flowing toward the sea of time

A river washes away children's laughter
Tumbling down the grassy bank
It gathers all the nameless voices
Into its gurgling composition
A symphony of endless moving water

A river washes away snow-packed slopes
Creates a cool drink of springtime
To refresh all the thirsty souls
And waiting mouths of eager men
Who savor all it has absorbed

To Rise Above

by Suzanne Bruce

Stature of pride as breezes
gently glide through slender
green needles   elegant height

magnificent pine extends
mighty branches grace
an azure sky   embedded

roots   strength of your splendid
trunk standing strong. I've even
seen snow bind to little limbs

dusted on larger cones
but you fight to remain in life
rather than give in   realize

how similar we are as I too
have reached to rise above
the forest only to find

wide distance   frightened
use incense from your wood
to pacify my ghosts

excise my nightmares
as I lean against you now
please teach me to live as tall.

In the Cleavage of Buckskin Hills

by Ramona Lappier

Long shadows at sunset
nestle in the cleavage
of buckskin hills that blush
as if seduced by twilight.

The periwinkle perimeter of sky
thins and dims as the sun descends,
as the mauves and muted blues move in,
pressed by the steel gray night.

Darkness brushes the hillside
into soft black suede
until the cleavage disappears,
until a blanket is laid,
until stars above shimmer
and glisten like tears.

Tidal

by Karen Marker

My Walden is the ocean
where the tides rise
and fall, where freshwater
rainwater, saltwater meet.

Long ago I learned
to feel most kindred
with the crowds of herons,
sandpipers, egrets, gulls.

I may follow Thoreau's footsteps
at the Cape—he really did walk
along that strip of land
from Orleans to Provincetown—

or I may find the path the Miwok took
through Muir Woods along Redwood Creek
where the Pacific draws me to it
as if it's the place of my birth.

My body has been shaped by currents,
sea bottoms, hidden recesses, low tide's
receding waters that leave me holding
a collection of stories of once living creatures
I can't toss out.

Welcome Back Swallows

by Jane Russell

Spring is when the Swallows come,
   back to nest on my front porch.
The nest awaits them, firmly built
   with twigs and mud tightly packed,
neatly tucked above the light,
   empty, waiting for their return.

One day I see a pair of Swallows,
   circling round and round,
taking turns on the nest,
   warming tiny splotched, speckled eggs,
babies waiting to be born,
   droppings decorating my porch again.

One morning broken egg shells
   appear among the droppings,
hungry chicks have hatched,
   needing constant feeding,
little black heads with rusty throats
   poke above the nest, beaks open wide.

Parents protect them,
   circle in their watchful vigil.
Downy babies quickly grow
   until they fill the nest,
faces now have white stripes,
   marked with rust and black.

Small fluffy gray feathers
    begin to flutter onto the porch.
The fledglings are trying flight wings,
    wobbly, awkward at first,
then back to the snug nest safety.
    Soon they will be gone.

The swallows nest again,
    birth cycle repeats,
a miracle of nature
    I am privileged to watch
every year in the spring,
    when the swallows return.

After the Bloom

by Johanna Ely

A shriveled orchid blossom
placed on the black bookshelf.
Two petals have dried open,
almost forming wings.
Gone the silky magenta blush—
instead, mauve-colored veins
mark pale, transparent skin,
tissue-paper thin
in the afternoon light.
A tiny purple tongue lies curled and silent.
I touch the parched lips,
whisper prayers of longing,
the white petals stiff, exquisite—
as if I could gently wake
a dead flower,
or rouse a sleeping angel
with a kiss.

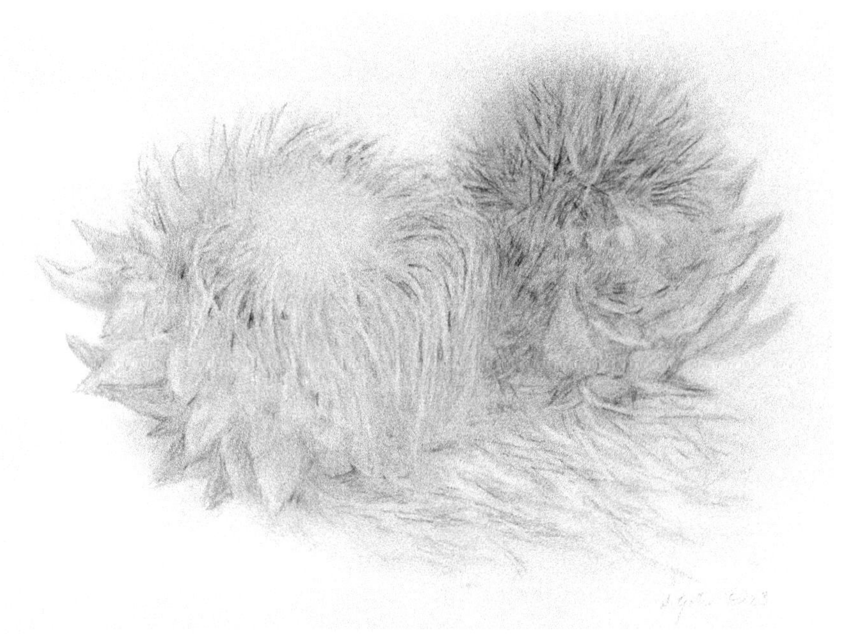

Two Old Blossoms by Sabina Yates, graphite on paper, 2023

Floating

by Johanna Ely

It is August,
the turning of a season.
I float in a space between
no longer and not yet.

Crimson dragonflies
hover and hum above a pond—
sip again and again
from a water lily's cup,
as if the petals will never close.

Giant monarchs
flit and flutter—
play tag in cloudless blue,
as if the sky will never end.

Amber leaves
that once were stars—
suspended and glowing
between heaven and earth—
drift in the afternoon breeze,
as if they will never fall.

A Beautiful Orchid Dreams

by Johanna Ely

Beautiful Phalaenopsis
dreams of being a fruit bat—
imagines its petals are ears,
rounded and soft,
able to locate the buzz of
a mosquito miles away—
how its bat face tapers into
a silky purple tongue,
a lovely place for honeybees to land—
to gaze upon a tiny white bud
who, centered among
luscious pink petals,
teases, whispers, *lick me.*

Beautiful Phalaenopsis
dreams a pollinator's dream—
flying all night,
bat wings stretched open like hands—
long tongue hungry for
the sugary nectar of desert agave—
nostrils craving the scent of
overripe mangoes.
Does it know that it has
a magenta face,
hue of a sensual blossom?
That a dream isn't just a dream—
or a flower just a flower?

In April

by Karen Marker

When we watched the brides take their time
circling round each other while the red-haired
woman rabbi chanted seven blessings and the brass
band played we knew everyone has a chance at joy.

Because April in New Orleans has the best weather
weddings happen every day. There's so much to love
in this city. It felt like only yesterday we heard the train's
whistle, the whirl of the plane, the long slow call of the boat
down along the curve of the river and took off
in the direction of music that's always somewhere
just around the corner.

Spring breezes give us a free pass, time to sleep
in the hammock all afternoon, get up like the birds
amassing in the mornings, listen to the mule drawn carriages
with their bells take the tourists down Burgundy, the drivers
pointing out the lattice on the single shot guns, the creole cottage

Even more festivals are coming interspersed
with miracles. The rising from the dead. The escaping
to freedom through a parting sea. Here we are rising up
like the cypress trees making new trees from knobs
in the grass under the long arms of the oaks, finding brown
speckled eggs fit perfectly into the palm of our hands.

Still we remember even in April disasters happen—
a volcanic eruption, a fire, a flood, an accident, everything
can be lost in a second. Or we may be saved
like the young woman by a bag of kumquats
picked earlier in the day from her father's tree,
strapped to her back, so when a drunken driver
slams into her bike they squish into the shape of her body.
A year later she's alive with a baby. And today
I'm starting where I am, from the beginning.

Snow Melt in the Sierra Mountains

by Karen Marker

At the summer solstice we stumble along,
sliding up and down the frozen banks
past pine needles tossed on white
like love letters winter brought.
Without footsteps to follow, we stop.

This snow is balm for the earth's scarred body—
snow that broke records, roofbeams,
glass in windows, roads and bridges
in Bear Valley, snow that toppled the trees
that block our way around
Alpine Lake and still holds on.
Deep in forest shadows it erases colors,
contours, plants, the path, all the damage

until the hot sun catches up and kisses the cold.
Drop by drop the snow melts like sugar candy.
Streams rush down from high above Bee Gulch.
The water's brush compresses rocks
with the sound of a trumpet's crash,
a melodica's rush of notes, a symphony
of ice and light that brings us close
as we can get to all that melts,
all that now heads fast into the raging
Stanislaus where the butterflies dance.

Sugar-rage

by Nancy Tolin

Scuffling hummingbirds
Fiercely territorial
Embrace Darwin's game
And furiously refuse
To share that backyard feeder

"I'm so tired," chirps one
"So am I," tweets the other
"Let's call a timeout!"
"We'll rest, sip some nectar—then
Resume our sugar-rage fight."

"Beaks like stilettos
Great for stabbing aggressors
In the throat!"—they laugh
"We're weaponized featherweights
Weighing less than a nickel."

High Flyers

by Kathleen Hermann

Orange swath lies across gentle slope
Tethered pilot sprints forward, rumpled sail lifts, puffs into
    crescent
Feet skim wild grasses, dangle above hilltops, skate into
    thin air
Over silver-streaked blue water, under wide open sky
Flying figure eights between sheer shoulders of the strait

Eye of the osprey holds strange bird in its sights
With slow, steady wingbeats, it scans the shallows,
    divebombs its prey
Asking only for safe return

Whale Encounter
by Jane Russell

Whale watching along
  the California coastline,
I was perched high above the ocean,
  on a craggy bluff with expansive view.
A pod of Gray whales appeared
  below in the aqua-blue sea,
moving with such grace,
  just under the sea glass,
rising to the surface,
  bodies so sleek and agile
for mammals of such girth.
  Weaving so smoothly
above and under water
  like needle and thread
slipping in and out of blue-green fabric.

Sea water spouted in geysers,
  fountains of droplets
exhaled in the air.
  Some breached above water,
exposing mighty flukes and fins,
  then spiraling downward,
while diving, sending huge splashes
  of white sea foam high in the air,
flukes fanned, then disappearing.
  I watched in awe until these whales
were out of sight, moving onward
  to their southern migration destination,
a perfect ending
  to a whale watch day.

Flight 1619, LAX to OAK

by Deborah Bachels Schmidt

Sunset was a band of subtle fire
between earth and sky,
quiescent embers on a bed of ash,
fading from lemon to green tea
to lavender and an endless wash of blue
beginning almost without pigment
and deepening to a Della Robbia glaze.
Through all the colors
drifted horizontal wisps of sooty cloud.

As we flew north,
the long sunset staying parallel
to the airplane's wing,
the blaze slowly cooled to russet,
and the dark ravelings of fog
lifted into the twilight.

The Pacific below was ruffled indigo silk
beaded with scattered clusters
of human lights,
small reflections of the celestial,
like diamonds at a woman's throat
catching the glow of the hearth.

As a child I imagined that each sunset
filled only *our* sky, *our* sea,
and that other people
must have their own sunsets.
I don't know how many suns
I thought there were.

But now I understood
the majesty of this radiance
limning the entire edge of the planet
as our hemisphere turns
toward darkness.

Balance

by Suzanne Bruce

Beguiling butterflies dart
                  around coastal bushes,
some white-winged,
                  others orange with black,
back on beach's edge
                  barnacles clinch sea rocks,
spellbinding sunlight
                  bounce off squally waves,
spirited foam surges
                  scatters shell pieces
as sand sinks,
          sticks between my tired toes.

To progressively stroll
                  periodically pause,
reflect remembrances,
                  ride the ebb and flow
of blight and bliss
                  beyond sneaky shadows
causing torrential tears,
                  visions torment feelings.
To precisely think
                  that bicyclists can balance
on two tires alone,
                  transient and smooth
wind whisks faces
                  like wishful desire.

Treasured thoughts flow
           timely hourglass poses
new quantum questions,
           to quietly fly, walk, ride,
or deeply dive
        to grasp or without doubt let go.

Usufruct

by Rob Rogers

"Your grandfather is ready to see you," the young man says. He is eager and earnest, with mud-stained shoes and a sunburned face. He is, she thinks, the kind of person her grandfather would have hired to work at the Foundation, and Dosia almost hates to have to correct him.

"That thing in the Visitor Center is not my grandfather," Dosia replies.

"Nevertheless," the young man says, "he's ready to see you now."

Everything about the cottage and the marsh and the beach between them looks so much as it did when she was a girl that Dosia can almost imagine the old man rattling around inside, staring through his magnifying glass at some wriggling thing he'd picked up on the sand. Which is exactly what she doesn't want to do. Her grandfather is dead, has been dead now for 16 years, and Dosia had lost the status of favorite granddaughter five or six years before that, however hard he had tried to convince her otherwise.

"Hello, Theodosia," the thing that is not her grandfather says.

"Where is the rest of the board?" Dosia asks.

"I asked them to wait," the old man says. "I wanted a moment to talk with my granddaughter."

"Machines don't have granddaughters," Dosia says.

"I suppose not," the old man says. "A machine only wants to keep going, whereas humans, all too aware of their own mortality, want to prepare the next generation to inherit the earth." He frowns. "And I want to teach this generation, and the ones that come after them, whom I'll probably outlive, that they're a part of this world, not its caretakers and certainly not its masters. So what does that make me?"

"A property owner who doesn't believe in property," Dosia says.

He grins, and Dosia has to catch herself—for a moment, she feels just the way she did when her real grandfather acknowledged something she had said or done was right.

"How long has it been since you've seen the property?" the old man asks. "You oughta get a sense of a place before setting out to destroy it."

"I'm not out to destroy anything and you know..." she snaps, but the figure in front of her holds up a hand.

"Sorry," the old man says. "Let me take you for a walk."

This stops her. "I didn't think you could leave this room," she says.

Her real grandfather, she knows, never entered this room, or any part of the Visitor Center. That had been built two years after she stood on the weatherworn floors of the cottage and taken her grandfather's wrinkled fingers in her own to squeeze them one last time. She had held on even after the old face had become still, past the point where the hospice nurse had asked her, with increasing firmness, to step away.

It had almost been a relief after that when the Terence Bramwell Foundation, the organization her grandfather had founded to carry on his environmental work, had asked the family for anything and everything related to his life: the birthday cards he had sent, his home movies, a recording of the interview Dosia had conducted with the old man in the eighth grade. She had wondered if someone within the Foundation was planning to write his biography, or even make a movie based on her grandfather's life. It had never occurred to her that all of that information would be fed into a computer's neural processor, would be indexed and cross-referenced and converted into an algorithm that would think and speak and act for all the world as if it really were the person she had wanted to grow up to become, in the days when doing so still seemed possible.

The figure snorts. "I'd hardly be in a position to tell everyone else what to do with these lands if I couldn't even go for a walk on them," it says. "They've given me a body, sturdier than the one you remember, that lets me gad about the place. I can even feel the sand between my toes. Give me a second to grab my stick."

This is not what she came here for. And yet the moment she breathes it in—the salt marsh tang, the smells of half-dried seaweed and black mud—she remembers how desperately she needs this.

"So tell me," the AI asks, "how it is you plan to save the world by building wigwams on the marsh."

She starts. She'd expected him—it—to let her take it all in, to walk a little of the path she used to follow with her real grandfather along the dunes, to enjoy herself before getting down to business. But that, she knows, was never her grandfather.

"The plan," she says carefully, "is to follow indigenous folkways…"

"Save the pitch for the board," the old man says. "Tell me what you want to do."

"I want people to live on the land again."

"In a nature preserve."

"On lands," she says, "that once belonged to the Ohlone and the Miwok. They were able to live on the land and be a part of it without destroying it. We can learn to do that again."

"The myth of the noble savage," the old man says. "I went through that phase myself when I was a little younger than you are. I still remember how disappointed I was to learn that people everywhere and at all times have always been just as selfish and destructive as they are now. The only difference is the scale of the damage they're able to do."

She can feel the eyes upon her, the tourists and true believers in flannel shirts and floppy hats staring at the apparition of the old man and his prodigal granddaughter pushing their way through the gray dunes. Yet all she cares to see are the things she has dreamed about in the only place she has ever thought of as home: a shearwater plunging into the waves and soaring up again with something shining in its beak, the cries of gulls and the gentle lapping of waves, the tantalizing flash of something here and gone in a rocky pool.

"When I was a little girl," Dosia says, "I would look out at all of this and think of this as the last place on earth people had yet to destroy."

"They've certainly tried," the old man mutters.

"I know," Dosia says. "I remember you telling me about the highway they wanted to build through these hills. About how farmers wanted to drain the marsh and run cattle along the dunes. I saw the pictures of harbor seals you brought into the courtroom when you were fighting to have this place preserved."

"That fight isn't something that took place 20 or 30 years ago," the old man says, giving her the look that used to silence her. "It's still going on, day after day, the greedy and the short-sighted circling like leopard sharks in the bay. And it will continue long after you and I are gone."

"But what you didn't tell me," Dosia begins, and the old man pauses, "was that all of those oak trees didn't just grow here by accident. They were planted and tended to by people who depended on their acorns. That the deer and the elk are thriving here because people thinned out the spaces between the trees and built a park for them to live in. And you and I both know that if we dug into one of these dunes—the ones you had me convinced "were laid down by God or glaciers, and not to be moved until one or the other of them came looking for them again"—we'd find hundreds of years' worth of oyster shells buried by the people who lived and ate and transformed this place into what it looks like now."

The old man continues to hold Dosia's gaze long enough to make her feel uncomfortable before softening.

"'By God or by glaciers.' I did say that, didn't I?"

"Often," Dosia says. They are past the spit now, the little strip of land that disappears at full high tide. There is less of it now than Dosia remembers.

"You also told me," she says, "over and over, that we are a part of all this. Not its caretaker, not its steward…"

"…and certainly not its master," the old man says. "I remember. Of course, these days they have that written on a postcard in the gift shop. Do people still send postcards?"

"When they want to make a point," Dosia says. "Do you know the last place I saw that quote? Someone had written it on the wall of a bus station in San Francisco."

The old man jabs his walking stick into the sand. "People will put all kinds of things on the walls of bus stations," he says.

"Nobody goes there to take the bus anymore," Dosia says. "They go there to sleep on the benches, to wash up in the one bathroom sink that's still working. To keep their children warm and dry on rainy days. The buses that run now? The ones going to tech companies in Mountain View and Menlo Park? They never stop at the bus station. We've separated ourselves so effectively that we've forgotten we're all supposed to be in this together."

"Maybe we've been telling ourselves the wrong story," the old man says. "We've convinced ourselves we're at the top of the food chain, but we've really always been at the bottom, scavenging like crabs for whatever we could get." He shifts his toes toward something small and sharp scuttling past them in the surf. "When the hermit crab runs out of room in his shell, he finds a bigger shell."

"We've done that," Dosia says. "I've done that, with your money. Built shelters in every place they would let me, always in those neighborhoods in those towns where the people in the tech buses will never have to see them. The problem isn't just finding everyone a place to live. It's reminding people there was a time, not so long ago, when people felt it was their responsibility to take care of each other."

He knows this; of course he knows this. Whatever program the Foundation used to bring a facsimile of her grandfather to life could surely calculate a solution to the problems of fractured communities and persistent inequality. She wonders if the AI is aware of that, if it ever feels the wasted potential of its existence in the way that she does.

"So you want to create a model village on the property," the old man says.

"I want to re-establish what was once here," Dosia says. "Built on site with sustainable materials, by people willing to take care of the land and each other. To show the world it could work. That it's possible. That's what this place is for, isn't it? That's why you still exist."

The old man considers this, placing one hand on his hat to keep the wind from blowing it away.

"You can preserve the past, but you can't re-create it," he says. "You could clone a mammoth, or a dodo, but where would it live? Once something is gone for good, it's gone forever. That's why it's so important to keep places like this the way they are, so that future generations..."

"What about the people who are here now, who will never be able to visit a place like this? People who have the same right to a clear sky and clean water and the feeling of sand in their toes as the rest of us, but who will only ever see it in one of your postcards?"

The old man raises his head. "Been to a public library lately?"

The question catches her off guard. "What?"

"Temples of learning. The intellectual heart of every community, more so even than the schools," the old man says. "Walk into one now, and you'll have to edge past the homeless people sleeping in the lobby. Or camped out in front of the computers. Or doing God knows what between the stacks. Is that what you want this place to become?"

The wind has died down now, and the air by the edge of the marsh feels salty and still.

"Sometimes," Dosia says, "I think the Foundation created you so that future generations could see what a cranky, prejudiced old man of the 20th century actually looked like."

"And sometimes," the old man says, "I remember that I created the Foundation because I no longer had the will or the energy to fight on my own for the things that are worth preserving. I knew I was getting older when I realized I had somehow gotten stuck with a reputation that I cared about. I didn't like it when people called me cruel to farmers, an enemy of progress, an old stick in the mud just because I wanted to keep their sticks out of my mud. I was getting sap-headed and sentimental and weak. Just like you."

Dosia flushes. "You think it's weak to care just as much for the people who have nowhere left to go as I do for keeping this beach the way it was when I was a little girl?"

"When you figure out how to make more estuaries, then no," the old man says. "When you can create something like this, something that supports so much life and adds so much in the world, then you can go ahead and fill it with all the wretched refuse of humanity you want. Because they don't seem to be in any short supply."

"You can't just freeze a place in time," Dosia says, drawing closer to the old man. "This isn't a museum. You have to allow the world to move on..."

"I have no power over tide nor storm nor glacier, and I can only honor what changes they choose to bestow," the old man says. "But I can stand fast against the developer and the despoiler. Even as well-meaning a one as my own granddaughter."

"You're not a person," Dosia says. "You're a relic, a clause in a dead man's will giving him unfair authority over the living. You're a ghost, playing the same tired old message for anyone who treads upon your hallowed ground. Except that you aren't even really here. You're on a server, buried on a hillside in Palo Alto, bringing this puppet"—she pokes the old man, sharply—"to life."

The old man slumps his shoulders, the water pooling around his ankles, and there is a moment when despite everything she has just said, Dosia wants to take the thing in her arms and hug it.

"I always knew the time would come when you would be disappointed in me," he said.

"I thought that was supposed to be my line."

He smiles, a little sadly. "You always undersold yourself," he says. "You've taken everything we ever did here"—he gestures toward the marsh—"and expanded upon it in the outside world. Truth be told, there are those on the board who believe you'd be a better choice to lead us into the next century than an old man whose best days were in the last one."

Dosia brushes his hand. "All I've ever done," she says, "all I've ever wanted to do, is to be someone my grandfather could be proud of."

The old man takes her fingers, squeezes them. "You've done that, and more," he says. "The hardest lesson the old have to learn is how to make way for the young. What was it Thomas Jefferson said? 'The earth belongs to the living.'"

Dosia bristles, knowing she should just let it go. Finally, she says, "The actual quote was, 'The earth belongs in usufruct to the living, not the dead.'"

"Usufruct?" the old man says.

"Typical Jefferson," Dosia says. "It's a legal term, related to land ownership. Basically it means that if you don't do anything to improve the land you're on—by European standards—then you don't deserve to keep it. It's the kind of reasoning that convinced him it was okay to steal the lands of the people who'd been living there for thousands of years."

The water is rising now, and Dosia wants to move further from its edge, but the old man continues to hold her hand.

"Jefferson didn't believe that the people he met or heard about—the Cherokee and the Mandan, the Shoshone and the Blackfeet—had done anything to improve their lands, despite all of the evidence in front of him," the old man says.

"He couldn't accept that maybe the people who had tended and shaped this land for a hundred generations knew more about how to take care of it than a sage on a mountain," Dosia says.

"For all his towering intellect, his curiosity, his farsightedness, Jefferson was still a man of his time," the old man says. "And he knew it. He thought the Constitution his generation had worked so hard to put together should be torn up every twenty years or so. Give the next generation a chance to work things out for themselves."

"'The earth belongs to the living,'" Dosia says.

"No doubt," the old man agrees. "Jefferson lived for 83 years, a ripe old age in his time, but a blip in the life of the land. How might he have behaved differently, I wonder, if he knew he would live to see the consequences of all of his actions?"

Something uncomfortable begins to wrinkle at the back of Dosia's mind. She struggles to remove her hand, but the old man has her fingers in a grip no human could break.

"You are one of the greatest lights of your generation, my Theodosia," the old man says, stroking her fingers with an affectionate gesture. "But a generation is all you will ever have. What you decide today, what the board decides today, will change the way these marshes and dunes will look to your grandchildren and great-grandchildren. And me. And I promise you, I will guide them and teach them, pass on everything I have learned to them, just as I did for you. And then I will outlive them."

"Get away from me," Dosia says, reaching out a fist to strike the old man—but the AI, anticipating her move, wraps her in an embrace, a fond grandfather holding his protege tight against the rising tide.

"You are no more qualified to decide the fate of these lands than a mayfly is to redecorate the human home where it lives and dies," the old man says. "The Foundation, the same board that took an oath to preserve these lands, they might agree with you. They lack the clarity of vision that comes with immortality. But they will never get to hear your proposal."

His face twitches, distorts, becomes for a second the grandfather she knows and versions of himself she has never met, before reverting, finally, to the gray faceless thing she has always known was underneath. The arms around her remain strong.

"We're both going to die out here," Dosia says.

"This body will die," says several different iterations of her grandfather's voice. "But as you pointed out just a moment ago, I am not this body. And the earth will belong to the living."

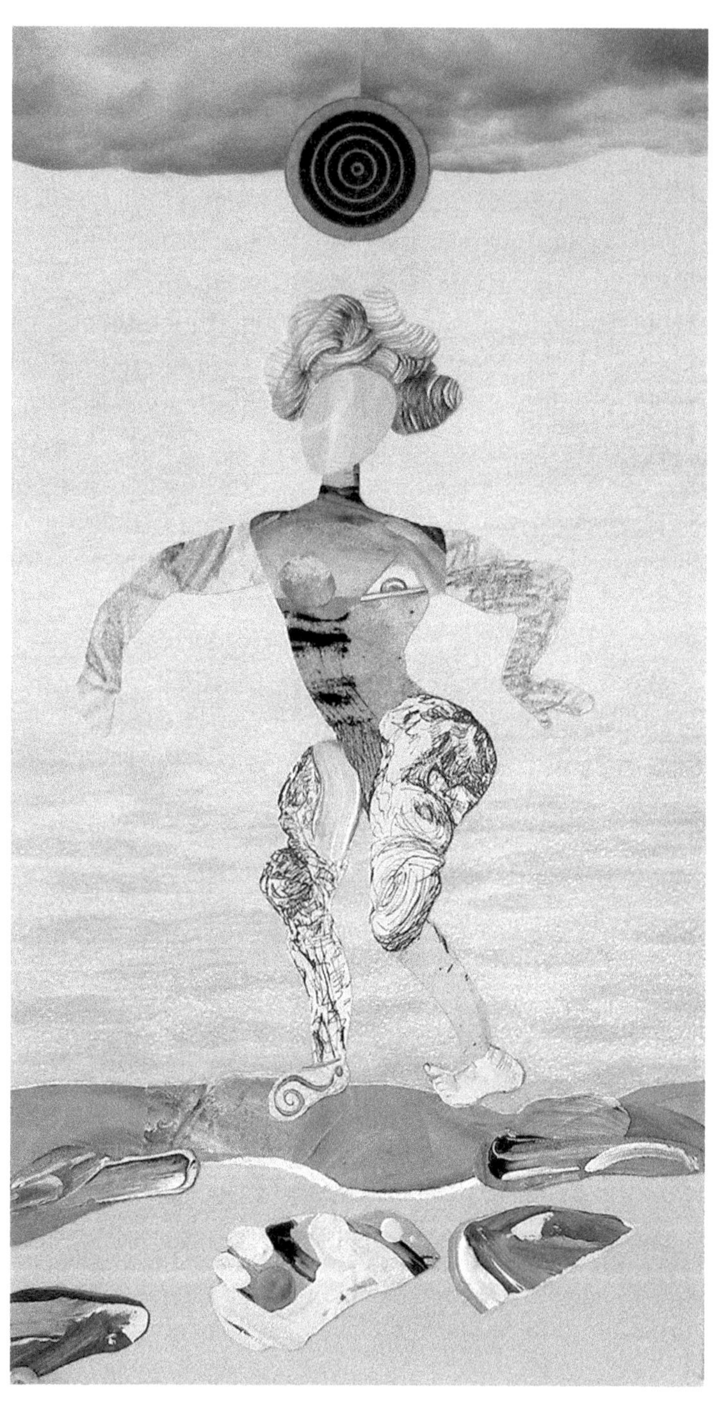

At the Beach by Diana Krevsky, mixed media
collage, 2009/2023

IV. Voices of Affirmation and Protest

Under Blue and Yellow Flags

by Sandy King

Air raid sirens wail. Miles-long caravans of enemy tanks move ever closer. Booms and earth tremors, rockets launched from far away. Bomb craters where busy roads once ran. Crowds await trains to carry them from danger. Unending lines of refugees walking, walking, walking, seeking safety in neighboring nations.

Many refuse to leave their homeland. Husbands and fathers take up arms to protect the beloved country. Mothers and children, the elderly and infirm, take refuge in basements and subway stations. Food and water dwindling daily. Civilians targeted and murdered. Apartment buildings fiercely burning. Churches blown apart. Hospitals ravaged. Wounded women, newborn babies rescued from a smoldering maternity hospital. Another rocket blast. Bodies of a mother and her two children lie on a once quiet street, their few possessions strewn about. A dog howls in fear. Neighbors bury the dead in shallow trenches. Diplomats talk but war goes on. Smell of gunfire and carnage lingers in the smoke-filled air.

May hope be found
In the destroyed church garden
Sunflowers still bloom.

The Risk of Spoken Yearnings

by Rick Hocker

I couldn't help but feel jealous whenever my older brother, Radwán, came home from school in the nearby town of Handar, Afghanistan. He would carry his books into his bedroom, close the door, and study until dinnertime.

Today, when he came out of his room, I said, "I want to go to school and study like you."

He laughed. "That's silly, Abida. Why would you need schooling? To do laundry?" He puffed his chest out. "I need to study so I can work and support my family someday." He pointed at me and said, "You will become someone's wife. Girls have no use for education."

"That's not true," I said. "Many famous women had educations."

"But they were not devoted to Allah or to their families. Those women only thought of themselves."

"I'm not like that. I'm devoted, but I want to better myself and learn."

"See? Already you are selfish," he sneered.

When my sisters and I washed our family's clothes at the local river in the cool mornings, I would talk to other girls my age about education while we pounded the clothes with wooden boards. My sisters would shush me, saying, "Don't talk about girls going to school. The Taliban has forbidden it."

"It's just talk," I said. "I'm not trying to change anything."

That night, my mother, sisters, and I served the men their evening meal in the living room. My uncle, Sherwanee, came for dinner as he did on most nights. His wife had died and he didn't like to cook. "It's women's work," he would say.

When the men had finished eating and we had cleared their table, we ate any leftovers in the kitchen while the men talked. Mother always cooked enough food to ensure leftovers for us. The kitchen was the domain of the women—the men never entered—so we enjoyed telling stories and laughing as we scooped lamb, rice, and vegetables onto flat disks of bread to reduce the number of plates to wash.

When Father appeared in the kitchen holding a small piece of paper, all conversation stopped. His eyes were fiery and damp. He said, "This note was slipped under our front door just now." He read the note to us. "Your daughter, Abida, has been poisoning girls with talk of education. Discipline her or we will be forced to silence her."

"Abida," Father said to me, "don't speak further to anyone about education. It will lead to more trouble and I can't protect you. I know you're a smart girl, but you're foolish in the ways of the world."

"What harm can I do?" I said. "I'm just a girl. I'm like a tiny mouse in a cornfield and I haven't even touched the corn. Is it so bad to dream about going to school?"

"Dreaming is dangerous for you, Abida. Now, promise me you won't speak of it again."

I looked down at my apron. "Yes, Father."

Three days later, while we were pounding laundry by the river, one of the neighbor girls approached me. The girl said, "Do you still believe girls should be educated?"

My sisters sent frightened glances at each other.

I decided that answering wasn't the same as bringing it up, so I said, "Yes."

My sisters' eyes became wide and they stared at me. "You should have said nothing," they chided me.

"I couldn't lie, could I?"

"Father won't like it."

"I did nothing wrong."

I went back to pounding clothes. When I looked up again, I saw the girl running toward our village. She disappeared between the buildings.

When we finished the laundry, we shoved the wet clothes into sacks and carried them back home. We walked through the center of town, as we always did, between the simple mud-brick buildings. The streets teemed with people and their animals, whose activity stirred up yellow dust on the dirt roads. We greeted the women we passed. We nodded to the men but didn't make eye contact.

A man moved into our path. We stepped aside. He moved in front of us. We stepped aside again and he moved in front of us again. When he was upon us, I looked up and saw a white cloth covering his face, except for his eyes. His eyes frightened me. I had never seen such fierceness and hate.

He bumped into me and something hot pierced my chest. I looked down and saw my dress stained with blood. I dropped the bundle of laundry. Then, I collapsed onto the ground like a fabric doll.

As my vision grew dark and my consciousness faded, I knew I would never see home again. I felt no fear or release, but wondered if heaven had schools for girls.

Passover, 2023

by Nancy Haskett

Perhaps the horseradish
was partly to blame,
flavored hot instead of our usual mild,
extra spice around the table.

Or maybe
it was the exodus story, itself,
a promise of freedom,
I will bring you out...
from darkness to light.

Whatever the reason,
sometime between singing *Dayenu*
and eating the meal,
both twins, still months away from turning seventeen,
felt it was appropriate to announce
that they are identifying as gay.

The Haggadah
has no script for this,
although it does emphasize multiple times
that many have suffered
under burdens of malice and ignorance
and tells us Elijah the Prophet
will turn the hearts of the parents to the children,

and so,
after this revelation,
after a few questions and answers,
we simply returned to the story,
took turns reading the narrative,
ate matzoh, charoset, and bitter herbs,
reminded, once again,
that we will continue to support all who are not free,
that we have an obligation
always
to be messengers of justice
and tolerance.

Big Business

by Nancy Haskett

Every two years,
the world's largest arms fair
is held in the London Docklands,
a place to showcase all the latest weapons.
Unlike a small-time gun show,
this event is not open to the public,
registration is limited
to the military or defense support businesses.

Attendees are usually well-dressed
in suits, blazers, ties, dresses, heels and pearls,
some in camouflage, some in uniforms,
some who wear robes and an Arabian *shora* on their heads,
many from international companies
such as Lockheed Martin, Boeing, BAE Systems.
They meander down crowded aisles,
admire exhibits displayed under bright spotlights—
tanks, missiles, bombs, armored trucks,
grenades, drones, robotics, tear gas—
or lunch at tables outside,
view helicopters and state-of-the-art naval vessels.

Mannequins pose with assault guns and rocket launchers,
noted speakers give lectures and workshops,
live models offer champagne, beer, and selfies,
while sales reps at various booths offer freebies
like stress balls shaped as bombs and grenades,
condoms packaged with the slogan,
The Ultimate Protection.
A string quartet, arranged on the back of a military truck,
plays Mozart,
one more attempt to add class to this festival of destruction,
this display of power
where everything offered
is for one purpose
only.

Looking for America

by Nancy Haskett

I'm empty and aching, and I don't know why,
Counting the cars on the New Jersey Turnpike,
They've all come to look for America.
                          —Paul Simon

America,
how did you get lost?
We were all together,
walking toward the same destination,
holding hands, marching, singing,
until you let go, turned the wrong way,
and we were pulled apart,
separated.

It happened so fast,
but obviously we weren't paying attention,
weren't watching you carefully in the crowd
among all the yelling and distractions;
one minute you were there,
and then we lost sight of you.

Our biggest fear
is that you've been kidnapped by domestic terrorists
armed with guns and disinformation,
false patriots who refuse to hear the truth,
will stop at nothing to thwart justice,
hold you hostage.

But perhaps
you have simply lost your way,
turned right when you should have gone left.
Maybe you can retrace your steps,
find your way back to where you started.

But if that doesn't work, don't worry;
lots of people are looking—
searching through empty promises,
abandoned ideals, wasted opportunities, lost causes,
unfulfilled dreams—
and we will find you again
somewhere.

Black and White

by Mary Susan Gast

Southwest Michigan, 1953

We lived on Townline Road. Out in the country. Dusty little farms everywhere.

Most everybody's grandparents came from Eastern Europe. We were Poles and Germans, Czechs, Slovaks, and Bohemians—as in "from Bohemia" (although now that I think about it, the Bohemians *were* the rowdiest of the neighbors).

There weren't many children living nearby when I was a kid. Summers were hot and lonely times for me. I hated the boredom and duress of picking berries and vegetables, squatting and stooping, swatting bugs and sweating day after week after month.

And I knew that all this effort wasn't even very profitable. I heard my parents talking at night about the cost of baskets and fertilizer and plants, and about the low prices fetched by the gorgeous and life-invested fruits of our labors.

The summer when I was just out of second grade—on my way to third whenever the cool solace of September finally arrived—my dad was downright angry about the tomatoes. "It's not even worth the gas to haul 'em to market," he said.

I was relieved to overhear this. Maybe we could just let them rot in the fields and I could sleep in mornings or wander through the woods across the road or play with my dog for the rest of August.

But the next morning at breakfast he revealed a plan. "Davis, at work, had an idea," he told my mom, his low, slow words clearing their way through the thick smells of eggs frying and coffee dripping in the last moments of cool, before dawn. "He says folks where he lives'd be real happy to buy fresh tomatoes from me."

On Saturday morning we loaded the 1936 Dodge pickup with old sagging peck baskets of luscious tomatoes. Tomatoes are heavy to lug around, but they aren't real hard to pick—no thorns, no bristles, easy to see among the green vines—so I didn't much resent the work involved. As he half sat on the worn leather seat and adjusted the strap of his overalls, Dad said to me, "Wanna come along?" "Does Mr. Davis have kids?" I wanted to know. "Sure," Dad said. So I climbed up into the passenger side where I'd have to look out through the cracked place in the windshield. But I didn't care. I was off to Buchanan and I'd be with kids. I unrolled the cuffs of my jeans and brushed out the sand that had accumulated, then rolled them back up.

Buchanan was where the factory was. My dad would get up around 4 in the morning, do some chores, eat his two fried eggs and white bread with butter, and be at work by 7, carrying his black lunch pail with hot coffee in the thermos. Unless they needed him to come in earlier. He was home by 4 in the afternoon. Unless there was overtime. Usually we'd eat supper at 4:30 and then he'd work on the farm.

His life at the factory was mysterious to me. He operated a core drill. I knew that, but I didn't have any idea what a core drill was. Sometimes there'd be a strike, which we all feared, but I didn't know why. I asked about it once and my mom (being the parental spokesperson) replied that it was "a terrible thing." So I assumed it was something like a flood, which I'd seen pictures of on the TV news shows. When there was a strike my dad didn't work, but he went to the factory at odd hours, to picket. A couple of times my mom and I brought his lunch pail to him when he had to stay longer at picketing. I'd just barely see the bunch of men standing around by the factory entrance,

as my mom eased our green Chrysler into the parking lot and
handed the lunch pail to the guard. "It's for Charlie," she'd say.
I'd wave to the guys on our way out, but I couldn't always tell
which one was my dad.

Two of my aunts lived in Buchanan, one in a teeny house
by the river, one farther into town. Any trip to a city was a big
deal for me. I couldn't for the life of me comprehend the abso-
lute blissful good fortune of people who got to live so close to
other people and stores and movie theaters AND who never
had to do farm work.

We drove along not talking. It was paved road most of
the way. The tires hummed. The chrome door handle on my
side rattled. The driver's side door didn't have a handle on the
inside; my Dad always had to roll down the window and unlatch
it from the outside when he wanted to get out. His arms were
so long, though, that it wasn't even a stretch for him.

I looked out the window on my side at the green trees and
the curving hills, at the apple orchards, and the grape vineyards
just getting ready to produce. I looked to my left at my Dad
every once in a while. He had one huge browned arm out the
window, his right hand managing the steering wheel, thumb
braced against one of the struts linking the outer rim to the horn
in the center. He drove with his thumb cocked way far back like
mine does. I played with my thumbs for a while.

As we got closer to the river the road curved more. I won-
dered how my Dad knew how to get where we were going. Even
though I'd been along these roads lots of times I could never map
out how to get to Buchanan. Finally we saw the St. Joe river. The
water was murky and you could tell it was running strong and deep.

Then, when we were just about into town, we turned
off the paved road. There were lots and lots of houses, close
together with lawns in front, built on crisscrossing dirt roads.
The houses looked like city, though the roads looked like
country. Most of the houses were about the size of ours, some
smaller. But the colors! I didn't know houses could be those

colors: deep purple and peony pink; butter yellow with chartreuse trim. "Here's where the colored folks live in Buchanan," my dad said. ("Colored" was considered the polite term in those days, and we used it.)

We pulled into the driveway of a dark green house, our old pickup providing the only sound except for a distant barking dog. A man with black skin came out the front door right away, smiling, his hand stretched out in greeting. My dad was already opening the door with his left hand from the outside of the truck. He swung his legs out and stood up. The two men shook hands and then walked on the crunchy driveway gravel to the back of the pickup, talking about tomatoes.

Soon—silently and fluidly—people were walking down the road to the dark green house, carrying empty paper bags and baskets, coming to buy tomatoes. My Dad hauled and lifted baskets. People picked out tomatoes and stayed around to talk. I was so busy watching out the open window on the driver's side of the cab that I jumped when someone rapped on the door on my side. The man who lived here—I surmised it must be Mr. Davis—said to me that his daughter, Merlena, was coming out soon so she and I could play.

As he finished speaking the front door opened again and a girl of 8 or 9 wearing a green and red plaid dress bounced down the cement steps and over to the pickup. We grinned at each other as I got out the door. We played all morning while my Dad sold tomatoes and the day heaped up its full allotment of heat and bright sun. We were in the house and in the yard. We tore around the blocks with 10 or 12 other kids. We chased her little brothers away. We drank Kool-Aid from blue plastic mugs and made puffs of dust rise by playing Slapjack in the driveway.

When the tomatoes were all bought, Mr. Davis and my Dad drank coffee in the kitchen and then my dad and I started back for home.

A thousand questions filled my mouth like communion-wafer butterflies. I swallowed all but one. "Why do the colored people in Buchanan all live in just that one spot?"

There was silence before my dad responded—not an unusual thing. "Because the white folks won't let 'em live anyplace else." All the way home I wondered about the white folks in Buchanan.

Later I wondered about us white folks on Townline Road.

A Plea for Change
"In Honor Of Earth Day"

by Suzanne Bruce

I am divine air, the breath of the sky
No one can see but can feel my sacred spirit fly,
How golden eagles gracefully glide high
On freedom, rest on rugged mountain tops.
Nearer to the ground, tall grasses sway,
Opening their blades to sun-filled promises,
Rhythms zigzag unsyncopated cadence.
Once upon a time, there were no concerns
For the foreverness of this earth,
Endurance a steadfast security, a silent smile
And a sure life. But now, an injured sphere, no
Respect has left lungs gasping, breaths
Thrashing. Glaciers melting, oceans rising,
Hugging a tree no longer hallowed meaning.
Darkness looming over hope, streams of
Actions must reverse increasing catastrophes,
Yearning for global shifts, for impassioned repair.

The Very Essence of Democracy
by Gail Wasserman

On June 6, 2023, I spent an evening at City Hall
Wasn't expecting to see much at all
I came to request Council Members reconsider
Funding for human resources, arts, and literature

Wow! What a surprise!
I watched the very essence of Democracy
Unfold right before my eyes
And the will of the people come alive

The Council finished their motions
And then one could hear a lot of commotion
Those helped by the non-profits were lining up to speak
It took hours for the individual testimonies to be complete

On June 27th, Council Members took a vote
The proposed zero funding was revoked

Wow! What a surprise!
I watched the very essence of Democracy
Unfold right before my eyes
And the will of the people come alive

America's Founding Fathers lying there in the clouds
Must be proud of our little town

Wow! What a surprise!
I watched the very essence of Democracy
Unfold right before my eyes
And the will of the people come alive

RBG and Me: A Memoir of Fashion Dysphoria

by Tamar Enoch

I will never forget the first time I saw her. I was flipping through the pages of the Sunday *New York Times Magazine* on Halloween morning, 1993. There, in the "Style" section, of all places, was a glossy color photograph of The Honorable Ruth Bader Ginsburg, taken on the day she was sworn in as a Supreme Court Justice. She was standing on the steps of the Court, wearing a jacket in my favorite shade of moss green. Her straight brown hair was parted down the middle and pulled back into a ponytail, almost the same way I wore my hair. She also wore glasses, as I did, instead of contact lenses, even though, according to the conventional wisdom of the time, glasses made a woman so much less attractive.

The columnist, Carrie Donovan, was lauding Ginsburg for choosing a tailored jacket for her first day at a new job, instead of one of the frilly fashion concoctions that were in style then. I gazed at the photograph in delighted disbelief. Could it be that a woman who looked and dressed sort of like me was being celebrated in the "Style" section of the *New York Times*? At the time, I was thirty-four years old and had just been appointed to a faculty position at a medical research institute. Like Justice Ginsburg, I was now at a professional level where women were very much in the minority. But, unlike The Honorable Ruth Bader Ginsburg, I had no idea what to wear.

I have hated wearing skirts and dresses for as long as I can remember. There was a time when girls couldn't wear anything else to school. I was an early rebel against this dress code. In 1969, when I was in sixth grade, I led a delegation of girls from my class to the principal's office, demanding to be allowed to wear pants when the weather was cold. We were sick and tired of freezing our asses off in the biting chill of the Kansas winter. Of course, that wasn't the vocabulary we used, but that was the point.

"I sure like seeing you girls in your skirts," Mr. Rice responded, after listening to our demands. He was almost pleading.

We countered that his pleasure came at the risk of our hypothermia. He hemmed and hawed, not sure what to make of this sudden flush of feminist radicalism at Pinckney Elementary School.

"We can learn just as well in slacks as we can in skirts," I piped up as we faced off across the impasse.

"Okay," Mr. Rice conceded, "if the temperature is below 32 degrees in the morning, you can come to school in slacks, but they have to be nice slacks. When it's warmer, I want to see you girls in skirts."

We marched out of the office in triumph, but our unity was short-lived. As soon as we were out of earshot, Mary Houston began to giggle, and soon the rest of the delegation had joined in.

"I'm glad we get to wear slacks when it's cold—but that part about learning no matter what we're wearing—how did you come up with that, Tamar? Girls are supposed to wear skirts and dresses. Are you trying to be a boy or something?"

Advocacy to keep our butts from freezing was one thing—interrogating the underlying rationale for gendered clothing was a horse of a very different color.

By then I had begun to wonder if there was something strange and different about me. Unlike many girls, I couldn't stand pink. I still don't like it. I also didn't share the urge so many of my friends had to dress up in flowing skirts, fluffy tutus, and our mothers' high heels. I did admire Glinda, the Good Witch of the East, but it was her magic powers I yearned for, not her rosy gown and golden curls. She was one of the few role models I had of a powerful, independent woman.

It wasn't that I wanted to be a boy. I was scared of fights, I was terrible at sports, and I adored cuddling animals. As I grew older, I had terrible crushes on boys and thrived on those long meandering conversations I could only have with other girls. But I continued to loathe getting dressed up. I just couldn't understand why I had to try to look like someone else's idea of beautiful. My older sister loved clothes and saved her allowance for shopping sprees. She chose cute mini-skirts, flowered bell bottoms, and puffy-sleeved peasant blouses—it was the sixties, after all. I was stuck wearing these outfits once she outgrew them. I didn't like them, but I didn't know what I did like, so I couldn't find the words to object. And, anyway, my thrifty mother wasn't going to invest in separate clothes for me, when there were perfectly serviceable hand-me-downs available.

I came to hate Halloween. As far as I was concerned, I had to wear a costume every day, so there was nothing exciting about putting on a different disguise. I went along with it for a while, because, like any kid, I loved that treasure trove of candy. Then, one year, I somehow ended up in a pumpkin fairy costume, consisting of a cardboard pumpkin strapped to my front and gauzy orange wings attached to my shoulders. There was also an orange wand I could wave around, just in case anyone wasn't instantly enchanted by the sight of me. I lasted less than a block in that get-up. After that night, I gave up trick-or-treating forever. I just couldn't walk around wearing things that made me feel gross and weird, even though it meant no more Tootsie Pops.

By the time high school started, the dress code had become much less prescribed. I could wear T-shirts and jeans to school every day, supplemented with a men's flannel shirt when it was cold. This continued to be my basic outfit through college, then on to grad school in biochemistry, and, finally, a postdoctoral fellowship in microbiology. I reasoned I had an airtight excuse not to dress up for work, since I handled corrosive chemicals regularly. Even after my faculty appointment, I couldn't manage a fashion upgrade. I hoped, perhaps naively, that I would be judged by my data, not my wardrobe.

As a scientist, I was not the only woman who eschewed a feminine presentation. While my personal style put me on the unfashionable end of the spectrum, it did not make me especially remarkable. With hindsight, I wonder how much of my freedom came with my white skin. As a white woman, I was respected and perceived as non-threatening no matter how I dressed, a privilege I took for granted. A woman of color, on the other hand, who could be ignored, shadowed, or profiled even when dressed to the nines, would have been taking on a whole different set of risks by dressing the way I did.

Sadly, my days of wardrobe freedom were destined to end. At the age of forty-four, I embarked on a new career as a speech therapist, inspired by my father's recovery from a debilitating stroke. It was a risk to make such a drastic midlife career change, but I took it joyfully. I wanted to work with people I might be able to help instead of test tubes. What I did not consider was the implications of moving from a male-dominated profession to one that was almost entirely female.

As a speech therapist, I had to set aside my jeans and T-shirts once and for all. I knew I needed to look "professional," presumably so clients would trust me, but probably more to signal the other "speechies" that I belonged in their tribe. Getting dressed each day turned out to be more stressful than teaching surly autistic teenagers. No matter how many clothes there were in my closet, I never had a thing to wear. Many mornings found me standing in front of the mirror, weeping tears of anxiety as I tried on and discarded outfit after outfit. I would end up throwing something on in desperation, just so I could leave home in time to get to work.

After years of agony, I gave up trying to look fashionable. I acquired five different oversized shirt jackets and assigned one to each weekday. I learned to throw the jacket of the day over a navy or black shell and dark pants without stopping to look in the mirror. I still had no idea how to apply makeup nor the interest to learn, and hairstyling for me consisted of brushing my hair and tying it back out of my face in a braid or a ponytail. In contrast, my colleagues were all elegantly dressed and coifed. It was a mystery to me how they found the bandwidth to plan the lush variety of outfits they wore to work, day after day.

My work as a speech therapist was emotionally rewarding and I came to love many of my clients and their families. And yet, for some reason, I felt ill at ease in professional circles. I changed jobs often, never staying at any position for longer than two years and never receiving any invitations to rise through the ranks.

Looking back from retirement, I wonder if my wardrobe was part of the problem. Most of my bosses were the kind of spiky-heeled power women who wouldn't be caught dead in a supermarket without makeup. For some reason, this kind of woman seems to be drawn to Special Ed Administration. Did they experience my dowdy gender-concealing style choices as some kind of subversive political statement? Were my colleagues unable to bond with me because I couldn't chat about cute shoes? Was there some kind of profound cultural incompatibility lurking just below our conscious awareness?

Meanwhile, I had started spending time in Buddhist monasteries on my vacations. In these settings, what to wear was strictly prescribed and shapeless. It was such a relief to put on the same thing day after day, and to have it be a unisex black, brown, or grey robe, depending on the flavor of Buddhism. Priests, nuns, and monks, who ruled the roost in monasteries, all sported shaved heads instead of hairdos. It was my idea of nirvana: a world where I didn't have to worry about making a fashion statement. Too bad monasteries don't hire speech therapists.

In these last few years, transgender and gender non-binary folks have finally started the conversation about gender expression that I couldn't have back in sixth grade. They are insisting that the human experience of gender does not always fall neatly into either the "masculine" or "feminine" boxes and does not necessarily correlate with a person's sex chromosomes. It's as if all these years we've been told there are only two colors in the world, pink and blue, and if you're assigned the female gender at birth, pink is the color you get.

I'm starting to believe I just don't have the right genes to feel comfortable in the clothes I have been expected to wear all my life. People who feel themselves to be in the wrong body are said to have gender dysphoria. What if you feel you are in the wrong clothes? Is there such a thing as fashion dysphoria?

Which brings me back to my first fashion heroine, Justice Ruth Bader Ginsburg. She passed away in September 2020, a few months after I retired from speech therapy. She had continued to wear glasses and to tie her hair back in that plain ponytail for the duration of her storied career on the Supreme Court. Hair scrunchies were her favorite fashion accessory. I've looked through scores of pictures of her, and I can't find a single one of her dressed in pink. (Her replacement, Justice Amy Coney Barrett, wore pink to her confirmation hearings.)

By the time she died, Ginsburg's approach to fashion had become iconic. That Halloween, there were women in RBG costumes everywhere. My neighbor was RBG. My three-year-old cousin was RBG. So was the cashier at Trader Joe's. That night, I dreamed I was parading through the streets of my old neighborhood costumed in my favorite jeans and a loose-fitting cotton T-shirt. I went from door to door shouting "Trick or Treat" and was greeted with cheers and smiles wherever I went. And soon, my bag was filled to the brim with Reese's Peanut Butter Cups, Tootsie Pops and Hershey's Kisses.

Cold and Bitter

by Evie Groch

Tea, beverage of choice for discomfort,
angst, fear, the need for self-care, tenderness.
It sits before me on the kitchen counter to help me
find the calm in eddies of hate, vitriol swirling down
the drain of human chaos around the globe.

I pray my tepid tea will counteract my dread of viruses
of religious certainty that foster tyrannical beliefs,
beliefs bathed in certainty the almighty speaks only to
and through privileged ones, teaches them
those who differ are condemned to hell.

My islet of calm is shrinking, my tea cooling.
Bleakness steals bits of relief right out from under me.
Climate is deflating any high spirits I hold.
I swat at the memory of scenes of devastation like
I would at an annoying bug.

I cannot cocoon myself enough,
crack the code for entry into conjuration
where magic might make things right.
Like a rattlesnake in high desert, I still try
to shed my skin of anguish, leave it behind
with flotsam and jetsam in soiled waters.

Until then, if ever, I sit and wait,
struggle to survive, see sanity return.

My tea turns cold and bitter.

Remnants by Steve Barbaria, acrylic on wood panel, 2023

V. Arrivals

Family Lore

by Alyza Lee Salomon

This was the story I knew, as my parents
repeatedly related. We were fortunate
to have a relative, Tante Pepi, who
owned a store and was wealthy.

She put up money, *affidavits*, for my grandparents
to get out of Nazi-controlled Europe in the nick
of time—it was already the fall of 1938, and Grandfather
was released from Dachau—to come to the US.

But not only for *Omama* and *Opapa*;
She furthermore arranged affidavits
for seventeen more relatives.
She was wealthy and could do this.

So when Robert first contacted me
and introduced himself, I said, "I know exactly
who you are! Your grandmother was the
wealthy woman who rescued my grandparents!"

But cousin Bobby corrected the tall tale
I had been spoonfed, like the other
family stories, *bobbemeises*, with long
versions referred to as "the whole *megillah*."

His Grandma Pauline, the family
called her Pepi, was not wealthy.
Yes, she co-owned a tobacco store,
and by this time she was already a widow.
To set up the affidavits, she borrowed
the money from her business partner.

Well shut my mouth! *Ausgezeichnet! Unberufen!*
The legend can now be revised by the ragged,
humble truth! Yes, we are fortunate to have
had a rich Tante Pauline. She rescued
nineteen relatives, including my grandparents
who arrived in New York Harbor in August of 1939.

She was able to do this because although
her purse was modest, she was indeed
exceedingly prosperous beyond measure,
for she was blessedly gifted with a golden heart.

Muddy River

by Louise Moises

Rio Grande runs thin through downtown El Paso,
slimy, clay-colored, liquid boundary between two countries,
shallow water, easy to wade across. Mud sucks
at the rubber sandals of nine-year-old Rosita.
She arrives with her parents,
Mother and daughter with skirts
worn thin by their journey from Venezuela.
In a backpack, father carries precious documents
and hope. Both parents, schoolteachers
fleeing political upheaval. Behind them a wave
of bone-weary travelers surge up the banks.

Everyday hundreds flow into El Paso. No jobs.
No sponsors. No relatives in the states, still
they come. Border Patrol overwhelmed by numbers,
herd migrants into the processing center,
cold warehouse, twenty-four hours a day, neon lights.
Clear plastic bags issued for belongings.
Faces scanned, fingerprints inked.
Families in federal custody, criminalized,
locked in over-crowded rooms,
charged with wishing for a better future.

Multitudes released into swelling El Paso.
Authorities arrange for chartered buses,
send the problem elsewhere. Day after day,
fleets of buses depart for New York City, Boston,
Denver, Miami, Albuquerque, Philadelphia, Martha's Vineyard,
cities not on the water-stained paper maps of the confused
    travelers.
The Governor of Texas sends a packed bus to the District of
    Columbia,
a rebuke for the current administration.
But this is not a new problem.
Mayors of distant cities declare a state of emergency,
request federal funds.

The Rio Grande continues to be crossed,
the muddy river flows.

Inspired by an article in the New York Times by Megan K. Stack,
"El Paso Can't Do It Alone"

Abuelita

by Jonathan Watson

the centerpiece of a store filled
with lighter shades
of plastic dolls

in your bell jar, you will not be
threadbare or
disassembled

the little girls can admire your twin
white braids and bespectacled face
from afar

they will not lift your *huipil* and see
the scars on your
brown back

they will not pull its string and hear
the men crowing
when you crossed
over the border

they will not see the arm bruises painted
faintly beneath
your laced shawl

they will not smell the rich cinnamon
and yeast of bread
pudding on your
porcelain breath

they will worship and lavish you
with marigolds
and breadcrumbs

they will celebrate your chaste pain but
secretly be ashamed
of not knowing
anything of it

Martyr

by Jonathan Watson

She said I inherited it
from people forced
to be Jesus or Mary
as a means to survive

what for heirlooms
and lands when
struggles and burdens
are more prized

the seamstress started
a tapestry that future
generations don't have
the patience to weave

the housewife who
crocheted the webs
meant for a crawl
through the maze

the soldier that went
missing in action
before his country
could bury him

should the dreamers
be taught how to
proudly bleed from
calloused hands

and the degradation
endured to put food
on the table and
pennies in pockets

my burden was carried
and my loneliness is
a luxury that I will
gratefully accept

Les Voyageurs

Bronze sculptures by Bruno Catalano

by Deborah Bachels Schmidt

In Marseilles, the ancient port,
witness through millennia
to so many leave-takings and arrivals,
bronze travelers stride the breakwater,
each carrying a single small valise,
all they were able to save,
all that connects them
to who they once were.

They are fragmentary figures
of impossible weight and balance.
We see through them to the sea,
the hazy skyline, the lighthouse,
a passing tugboat. They seem
to be disappearing
from their cores outward.
The disappearing begins
with their hearts.

For despite the invitations
of glossy brochures
with their handsome captains
and radiant beaches,
many of us do not travel by choice.
We leave only because we must,
because life has become impossible,
and when we go
we leave pieces of ourselves behind.

We leave pieces of ourselves
with the slant of afternoon sun
across the harbor in Manila,
with the mynahs calling from the eaves
of our grandmother's house in Aminpur,
with the brother buried in Kabul,
with the lemon tree in the courtyard in Aleppo,
the tree no one will water now.

We leave pieces of ourselves behind,
and wherever we arrive,
we can never be quite whole again.

Empty Dress by Jennifer Lothrigel, photography, 2021

VI. In The Dying Season

Not Picking Daisies

by Beth Grimm

The children on the hill.

What are they doing?
Picking daisies? Hunting Easter eggs?
Where are their baskets?

9 and 9, 12, and 13
Innocence unblemished
Grab a baggie, follow the piper, Grandpa Will
Up the side of the landscaped hill.

One small hand drops dust among the flowers
Another daintily shakes the corner of the baggie,
Do I dare to touch?
One throws caution and the ashes to the wind
Oops...blowback...happens to the piper too
when at my call, he turns for a picture
Hand opens up...Great Grandma Iva,
All over his suit and newly polished shoes.
Everyone laughs.

What are they thinking?
Fun game...grab the baggies and run
Scatter the dust...no mistrust
No rules...no prizes...no competition
no medals...no trophy...
And they loved it anyway.

Innocence, childlike behavior
Joining in...being a part of something
On this a special day.

I will remember it fondly,
Not picking daisies but putting them back?
in a beautiful garden...with a memorial plaque.

And I'll see my mother, high up on a pedestal
Above the garden of my brother, gazing down,

A twinkle in her eye, a smile on her lips.

In The Dying Season...A Letter to My Father Who Thought People Were Here to Serve Him

by Beth Grimm

Now that you have the final sentence
Arteries closing...heartbeat slowing.
Do you think about your choices?
Search the silence for encouraging voices?
Do you seek out hiding places?
Retreat to inner spaces?
Are you impervious to the troubled faces?

With all the passing hours
Does it occur to you how little you gave?
How much you extracted?
When your harshly critical words
Made to rain on those who loved you.
How people still showed up.

As to those who gather 'round
Does their palpable grief set you aground?
How do you possibly cope?
Do you let it choke? Do you drown?
Do you count every heartbeat? Cherish every breath?
When you know it will slow at an agonizing pace,
and lead to inevitable death?

In this season of dying
Do you thank God for what you had?
Or damn him for everything bad
Much of which you brought on yourself.
Will you grope for some untouchable grain of hope?
Will you show fear? Or just contemplate
that inevitable, perturbable impending date.

In this season of dying
at the moment of death,
will you make a scene or remain serene.
When the time comes
Do you think you'll be able to hold your breath
And slip into a better dream?

Learning to Exit

by Peter Bray

We learn how to walk, talk, tie our own shoes,
choose Blue as our favorite Crayon color,
do some art and Mom or Dad
will hang it on the wall.
Times get harder, tougher, and we learn
how to get from the 5th grade to the 6th,
high school and College or Trade school,
maybe Grad School-UCB,
sweat on the brow now, our first job
and first layoff, how to recover,
lover or romance, arrive and try
to stay away from those Divorce Court Proceedings,
how much is lost to community property splits?
Once? Twice? Another layoff, children and Oh,
the river flow is deep and Oh so wide.
Empty nesters, the testers never seem
to de-escalate, but wait, we're declining in our vitality?
Walking with a cane, and where did my balance go?
What? We must now Learn How to Exit:
Who will go first? Is the Trust in order?
How much is the Social Security Survivor split?
How mobile will we be?
Long Term Disability Coverage?
How much equity is in the house?
Reverse Mortgage the rest?
Ashes in an urn or toss at sea?
But "Only at High Tide."
Or up on the Benicia hill
with a view of the Beloved Waterfront?
Who will do the tossing when two daughters

have already gone? Son Chris, Lela, & Tracy,
the next generation! What about
this house full of junk and Memorabilia-collectibles?
38 years worth? Begin downsizing now,
today, by the trailer load or to Goodwill?
Or the dump?

The Last I Love You

by Stacy Gardner

One

In the waning hours of daylight, between lunch and dinner, the restaurant was nearly empty. Jess took a seat near the back, slipped her purse off her shoulder and set it on the chair next to her.

The waitress placed a short glass of ice water and a tall menu on the white tablecloth. "I'll be right back to take your order." Jess hadn't eaten all day and was weary from bearing witness to everyone's emotions, not to mention having a few of her own. The drive home would take more than an hour. Stopping to eat in St. Helena seemed the prudent thing to do, given her emotional and physical exhaustion. The day had been long and arduous.

Jess arrived at the hospital that morning after her mother had been taken into surgery. Ange, who lived nearby, was already there. Jess and Ange spent the better part of the day sitting silently in the waiting area reserved for families of the very ill and dying. From there, they could see out the floor-to-ceiling windows across wine country. The sun was shining. The vineyards formed perfectly bucolic rows from hill to valley. In October, the weather in St. Helena was characteristically pleasant and warm.

It was mid-afternoon when the scrub nurse entered the waiting room and told Jess that her mom was finally out of surgery. Ange had gone home to see her family, eat, and rest a bit. Jess followed the nurse back to the ICU.

Jess's mother lay on the bed, a team of medical professionals surrounding her. Multiple machines beeped, and wires fed into her body from three sides. Only her feet remained unencumbered. Jess tried to make herself as small as possible, pressing her body into a corner to stay out of the way. Her mother was clearly in pain. The nurses were trying to make her comfortable, but nothing seemed to work. The doctor had already moved on to his next patient.

"Hi, Mom. How are you feeling?" Jess wasn't prepared for the response.

"Oh, God, Jess. You have no idea. No idea."

Jess hated the pain she heard in her mother's voice—she sounded small, frail, desperate, afraid. Even more, she hated herself for thinking, *This is so fucked up. You did this to yourself.* She felt pity and repulsion at the same time. *Fuck. Why couldn't you be like other moms? Why couldn't you have just taken care of yourself? Of us?*

Jess flashed back to her eleven-year-old self arriving home from school to find her mom passed out on the living room couch. Familiar feelings of chaos, insecurity, and hyper-vigilance surged through her body with such ferocity that the small hospital room suddenly became oppressive and tomb-like.

She couldn't get out of there fast enough.

"Okay, Mom, I'm going to take off so they can take care of you." Jess almost made it to the door when she heard her mother's broken voice call out, "Jess. Wait...Jess...I love you." She'd heard those words a million times, but, absent protection or guidance, they always felt empty. "I love you, too, Mom." And, with that, she walked out the door.

While Jess waited for the waitress to come back for her order, she toyed with the idea of having a glass of wine. It had been a stressful day (week, month, year) and her eyes kept returning to the extensive list of wines by the glass. It had been a year or so since her last drink. She also had a "zero-tolerance" policy about drinking and driving. So, when the waitress came back, Jess just ordered some food. It doesn't matter what it was. Jess wouldn't remember. What she did remember, years later, was that, the next time the waitress walked by, Jess smiled, apologized for bothering her, and ordered a glass of Duckhorn Cabernet. After all, she was her mother's daughter.

Halfway through the glass of wine and shortly after her food arrived, Jess's purse began to vibrate. She really didn't want to talk to anybody. "God," she thought, "I just want to finish my drink, my meal, and go home." Realizing that she hadn't updated Ange after their mother came out of surgery, she reluctantly pulled out her phone and checked the screen. Yep. It was Ange.

"Jess, where are you? They're taking Mom back into surgery." There was panic and urgency in her voice.

"What do you mean? I just left there. I'm still in St. Helena. What's wrong?"

"I don't know. I just got back to the hospital to see Mom and when I went to her room, they said she was being prepped for surgery. She's bleeding internally. They won't let me see her."

"Fuck. Okay. I'm coming back. I'll be there in about 20 minutes."

Jess put her phone back in her purse. She sat there for a moment before pushing her plate away. She finished the glass of wine and put her credit card on the table. The waitress obligingly brought the check.

Driving back up Deer Park Road Jess was struck by how beautiful and how dark the world could be at the same time. The wooded area glowed with the last of the day's golden rays, while an adrenaline-fueled tightness flooded her chest. She turned into the hospital parking lot at the top of the hill.

She found Ange sitting in the waiting area, a half-empty plastic water bottle on the table next to her.

"Did you call Kat or Tina?" Jess asked.

"No, Jess. I don't think I can. You better do it."

Jess again pulled her phone from her bag and stepped to the far side of the room to call the other sisters and give them an update. Fortunately, the barrage of questions coming at her could all be answered with "I don't know...I don't know." Because, well, she *didn't* know. She didn't know why, exactly, their mom was taken back into surgery. She didn't know how serious it was or how long it would take. She didn't know when the medical team would give her an update. She. Just. Didn't. Know.

After the second call, Jess remembered to start breathing again. She leaned against the wall, not so much to steady herself, but to rest. Stress and exhaustion were taking over. And just as her breathing started to return to normal, the elevator dinged and the doors clicked open.

"I'm Dr. Galvin. I'm looking for Ange or Jess Bennett."

"I'm Jess Bennett."

"Jess, I'm the surgeon who was taking care of your mom. As you know, we had to take her back into surgery a second time....*wah wah wah*...couldn't stop the bleeding...*wah wah wah*...tried everything we could...*wah wah wah*....so sorry... *wah wah wah*."

Jess stood there, listening to the doctor. She watched the exchange between them as if she were standing near, but not in, her own body.

"Can I see her?"

"Yes," Dr. Galvin replied. "Give us some time to clean her up. The nurse will walk you back when she's ready."

Two

Jess returned to the seat next to Ange. She watched quietly as her sister's face twisted and tears slipped through closed eyelids. Jess, the oldest, was accustomed to holding herself together. She never cried in front of anyone. Never. Ever.

She turned to Ange, the weight of the news landing heavy in her chest, "Oh my god. Oh my god." Ange's eyes fluttered open. "I can't do this," Ange said. "I have to get out of here." With that, Ange stood up, gave Jess a weak hug, and made for the elevators.

The clicking of the elevator doors closing was the only sound in the too-quiet corridor. Jess was, once again, alone, carrying the weight of death and loss. Carrying the burden of generations.

There was nothing else to do. She sat back down. She waited.

The pale green carpet beneath her feet was clearly chosen for its durability rather than its aesthetic appeal. She studied the faint lines that crisscrossed the acrylic loop and, in her mind's eye, traced the abstract pattern. After what seemed like hours, the elevator dinged, and then clicked again. A nurse in rumpled green scrubs, surgical mask hanging from her neck, approached Jess and asked if she was ready.

Jess dutifully followed the nurse. The soft soles of their shoes squished on the linoleum. The silence of the hall served to amplify every little sound—from the pounding of Jess's heart, to her too-heavy exhalations, to the monotone voices wafting down from the intercom speakers overhead.

After a series of heavy doors, empty halls, and signs that said, "No admittance. Staff only," Jess entered a small room surrounded by white curtains. White floors, white walls...even the various pieces of equipment lining the walls were white. Her mother's long black hair, stuck to her head in some spots and haphazardly splayed on the white pillowcase in others, offered the only contrast in the room. Even her pale skin seemed to disappear into the thin hospital sheets.

Jess stood there confused, unable to integrate the reality of what she was seeing into her previous expectations of the day. She knew her mom was having major surgery, but it wasn't supposed to turn out like this. But then again, why wouldn't it? Though only 72, her mother's health had been in decline for decades.

Jess's arms, her legs—everything felt heavy and awkward. She looked at her mother. The nurse had cautioned her that there would be a tube protruding from her mother's mouth. The law dictated that it was not to be removed until the coroner had done his examination. So, there it was, just a few inches of plastic attached to a coupler of some sort, causing her mother's mouth to gape into an unnatural "o." This was especially disconcerting to Jess, as her mother, having lost her teeth years ago, was always quick to cover her open mouth with her hand. Her dentures were ill-fitting, so she rarely wore them. The plastic pressed against her naked gums.

The frigid air bit Jess's exposed skin. She thought she could see the fog of her breath with each exhalation. Was it real, or was she imagining it?

"Can I have a few minutes with her?" Jess heard her own voice as though she were hearing a stranger speak. She didn't recognize the flat, faraway tone. Her mouth struggled to form the words.

"Take all the time you need," the nurse said gently as she disappeared behind the white curtain and, with a swish, left the room.

Jess watched her own hand rise and touch her mother's forehead. Where she expected to feel the warmth of her mother's skin, she felt instead cold flesh. The large round analogue clock on the wall ticked off each second. It was a metronome keeping time with death. Nothing else moved. Jess drew her hand back sharply, but not before forcing a whispered, "I love you, Mom." She felt self-conscious and inadequate saying the words. Her mother was gone. There was nothing left to do. Nothing left to be done.

The Old Baron

(Homage to a Shipwreck)

by Woodrow Shiftlett

My weary wooden bones rest in Carquinez mud
So distant from Ketchikan shores and fishing grounds...
Down Pacific, to 'Frisco Bay, moored in the Strait.
Young Jack, fish patrol indeed, reformed oyster pirates,
Plied these waters and relished dark runnings.

Time danced, Canadian bootleg filled my belly
Off-shore, Glen Cove by night
What parties at Stremmel's mansion!
Oh the times...

Sailing life waxed short
Old Joe sunk me, shielding Southampton shipyard from
        battering waves
Fading paint accented, white daubs
From dive-bombing gulls.
Yellow crane, my companion, nearby, stories told
Building Panama Canal...or Golden Gate?

Resting here where Benicia bordellos boomed once
I no longer see sunrise
Only sunsets' waning rays...
Marking muddy demise
Then am I again the Red Baron...

Tali/Medusa by Morrie Warshawski, graphite and tempera, 2023

VII. Character Tales

In the Kitchen

by Alyza Lee Salomon

When the ants show up, something is out
of sync—it might be the dishes
and food particles on the counter

or table-top, a reasonable surface
assessment, but in my experience,
there's usually a more profound disparity

as well, some under-the-rug crisis
that's crying to be addressed,
like a raining stream of misplaced anger

toward the one you know best,
or the unrequited desire to achieve
something not yet attainable. Love isn't

always the vehicle for meeting consciousness;
sometimes karma manifests as irritation,
a surfactant train of agitation that grates

and grates until cleansing takes place.
So rearrange the floor and designate a familial
Grand Central Station for healing:

Stare your hunger's slavish demon in the eye
and welcome home your biggest fear—then see
how sweetly the bugs flee and disappear.

Split-Second Judgment

by Nancy Tolin

Ah, the Gangway, with its nautical theme—that ever-popular watering hole in the Tenderloin. Governed by the traffic light, I frequently find myself stopped near this dive bar while driving to work. A ringside seat in this seedy neighborhood, a gritty vignette of early morning San Francisco. I watch the cluster of men, some standing, some seated on the sidewalk, drunk already—or were they there all night and are simply waking up to enter the bar again to be served by the morning bartender?

Bright cobalt blue walls greet these patrons. The vibrant blue gradually lightens overhead, then transforms into an ocean mural—one that sports a large, funky, beige ship's hull in 3D above the bar's entrance.

The Gangway's narrow sign climbs the six-story, century-old tenement building, perpendicular to the vintage railings and metal dropdown fire escapes. Large blue letters spell the bar's name alongside a thin, very tall, red cocktail glass. A rainbow flag hangs from the bottom of the sign, fluttering in the wind.

I wait for the light to change and watch a suited businessman walk out of the bar and stand near the curb. He takes a puff from his cigarette, then extends his arm, one hand holding his lit cigarette stub balanced between his two upright fingers, and with the forefinger of his other hand, he flicks the butt through the air and into the gutter.

A moment's judgment flickers across my mind as I watch this slightly intoxicated man who is now littering the street. But then, with split-second timing, a passerby runs to the gutter, grabs the lit stub, takes a long draw, then darts back onto the sidewalk, and happily walks away smoking what is left of the cigarette.

Freedom in Five Gears

by Stacy Gardner

Back the fuck up!
This car, she says, *doesn't go in reverse.*
I'm going. I won't be coming back.

See the shape of her words through the brown tinted glass.

Jamming into second, powering into third,
Torque pushes her bruised and bloodied back against the leather.
Fourth transitions to an effortless, flying fifth,

The final "*Fuck You.*"

Pale cheeks flash red with rage,
Spewing spit, he commands her return.

The teeny, tiny man disappears in her rearview mirror.

Self-emancipation at 110 miles per hour,
The pedal hasn't even reached the floor.
Hard driving bass reverberates through her body.

She races toward a freedom she's never known.

Johnny Cash's Victim

by Michael MacDonald

10:15 A.M., Reno

Some would say I got a problem. Me, I'd say I had more than just one problem, except I've got this middle name: Denial. So, no, no problem. Problems. Whatever.

Been up all night. Hittin' the Silver Legacy, my go-to base of ops, burning through another stake. Except for that last bet, lucky number... Hmm. Forgot. But I put my last 20—all that was left—on that lucky number whatever and, of course, having given up all hopes of having beer money, a dinner... Wham! Hits. Good ol' lucky number whatever.

So, played the dollar Blackjack tables a little, got a chunk back, then when the mood was upon me, moved up to bigger things. No—no problem, though. Totally under control. Like, I got rules. I stick to 'em. Numero uno: No drinking while gambling. Learned that one back when I thought I'd make my name on the poker circuit. No, I hold off on the drinkie-poos until I'm done gambling.

I'm done gambling now.

Having a drink.

In a bar.

Shooters, the name of the bar. Right across from the Silver Legacy. It's 10:20 A.M. And life's good.

Bartender's hunkering down, other end of the bar. Dunno if he's avoiding me. Like, who wants to talk with the sort of scuzz drinking in the morning? Those sorts have problems. Who needs 'em? Hey, me neither, bartender-oonie.

Been here before. Pretty much like this, A.M., tall cold one in hand, coming out a bit ahead on the night. So I know, another hour or so, place'll start getting a bit more lively. Night-shifters driving straight up from SF area, Sacramento, playing around a little on a weekday, the hell with sleep, night-shift blowing holy hell to a sleep schedule anyway, right? So, they scoot on up here, step into the bar for a not-watered-down quick shot or two, hoping Lady Luck's living in that warm cozy first-shot feel, before heading into the maelstrom of casino-land.

Anyway, if I was the sort to have problems, another one—that I don't have, of course—would be having a crap-ton of back child-support due. And I won't have that problem because I got enough to pay the ex; nowhere near gonna be paid up but it'll be enough to keep her from siccing the state on me, garnishing my "wages" such as they are. Whatever.

See, if I had a real job, that'd be another problem I'd have. But I don't. Have a job. Or have a problem.

Well, yeah. I feel like crap when I think about not helping out my own kid. That—now that might be a problem.

Or, hey, it would be for someone who indulged in that kind of negative thinking. We all know that negative thinking brings on negative things. Like negative luck.

10:15 A.M., Rest stop on I-80

Danny Dollar Boy swaggers out of the rest stop men's room, takes in the mountain air, the late-spring patches of snow on the ground, the bite of the chill that cuts through his threadbare hoodie but still feels good, alive. Takes in the fact that he's truant once again, job be damned. Sonsabitches have him on a "plan" anyway, like they had any right to be getting in his face about a lousy argument or two with the dickhead white-collar weenies diddling their laptops and looking down on people who worked for a living—like the building maintenance crew. In particular, him, Danny Boy, in other words.

Oh, well, tough titty. Better days ahead, right? Danny thinks. *Anyway, today's a better day. And where'd everyone go?*

Car parked right in front of the restrooms, nobody there. But Danny hears some grab-ass laughter off to the left. so he carries his swagger that way, see what's up.

He walks past the women's restroom towards the sound of the guys. And Janice. Laughing. Past the log cabiny-looking building housing the bathrooms, past the little shelter for the vending machines selling stale candy and past-expiration-date sodas. They aren't at the first of the weird concrete table-and-bench things, but about 25 yards beyond, at that one, alongside the parking lot.

Beyond them pine trees tower overhead, but the table is in a little notch of clearing, past a path that leads away from the parking lot. Somewhere the mom-'n-pops would let the kids out to burn off some of that energy from being cooped up, or let the dog out to do its business, handy doggy-poo bags in a dispenser right at the beginning of the path. Sierras, wild and big, but here, pretty well tamed. Just the last rest stop for the next 40 miles or so, the sign back a-ways said. Another hour and a half or so and he'd be in Reno. Party-time!

Janice was sitting up on the table, Bob and Jim standing next to the table. And Janice. All of them laughing about some ass thing. Danny says, "Hey, what'd I miss?" They get all quiet.

"Hey, man," Jim says. "Just hangin'. Ready to go?"

Janice: "Hey! Wait! Let's go see where that trail goes." She's pointing back at the little path Danny just had walked past.

Bob says, "Hoo-yah! Nature gurl wants to go all wild on us here!"

Janice rises to the taunt: "Yeah, you wouldn't know what to do if I went all wild on you, City Boy!" Jim cracks up, Bob blushes—an implicit admission that she's probably right.

Danny's looking at Janice like full of Ouch!, glares at Jim and Bob, then says "My family used to stop here on the way to Tahoe. The trail just winds around out back of the bathrooms and then comes out at the parking lot for the truckers. Let's just get going."

Jim tucks his thumbs in the waistband of his jeans, swaggers, and drawls, "Ya know, Ah think Ah'm a-gonna mosey on down the trail, see if I can rustle me up some bar meat." He starts back to the trail, in kind of parody of a bow-legged cowpoke.

Bob laughs and follows him, but comments, "The hell, Jim. You a cowboy or a mountain man? Living on pine nuts and trapping beaver or the hell what? Huh?"

While the boys wander off down the trail, Janice turns to Danny. "What's got your knickers in a bunch?"

"Me? What about you? Gettin' all flirty with them, and I thought we'd just be coming up here together."

"We are together... What's the matter? Jealous?"

He looks away guiltily.

"Oh, come on. I've known them since I was in third grade. We're just friends. Really, you got nothing to worry about with me."

"Maybe. But still... You are kind of flirty with them."

"Just kidding around. Hey, lighten up. Try to have some fun." She jumps off the table, gives Danny a quick peck on the cheek and bounces on down the trail. Shouts after Jim and Bob "Hey, guys! You assholes trap any beaver out there? I'm coming down there to count your furs, Ha-ha!"

Danny Boy Dollar watches her catch up to her "friends," then go around a turn and out of sight. Eyes the trail like it was a path to pain and doom, turns around and slowly walks over to his car, leans on the hood for a minute or so, waiting. Then gets in the driver's seat, leans over to open the glove box.

Takes out a couple papers, registration, owner's manual. Then, a pistol, .38 Special. He mumbles, "Hey, Dad. Might need your help. What do I do about Janice? She's the one for me, but keeps fooling around with anybody she sees."

Waits for something to come to him, some sage advice.

Nothing happens, though. He puts the gun back in its place, covers it with the papers, closes the glovebox.

1:15 P.M.

I'd managed to cop a pretty good buzz, figured, Hey! Time to see what Lady Luck has in store for me these daylight hours. So I wandered back across the street to the Silver Legacy, and you know what? Still had the mojo working, took just a little over an hour, until about 15 minutes ago, to bump the stake up by a couple grand.

Don't get all google-eyed, there. Not to say I had a problem, but I was in debt seven ways to Sunday school in hell so couple grand's just... investment money, you might say. Bumping up my investment in my little gambling sole proprietorship.

So, back here at Shooters. And, true to form, still not touristy-weekend crowded at all, but smattering of folks celebrating Tuesday with me.

I'm sitting at the bar towards the back, straight shot to the double-glass doors glaring with a halo of afternoon sunshine. And in walks three people. Hard to make them out against the glare, but as they come into the place, they're easier to see. To see that they're just kids. Hey, not that I'm ancient or anything, but you guessed it, wise beyond my 28 years.

Anyway, there's two guys kinda huddled together like secretly plotting a next move; looking guilty as all hell. Another guy lurking in back, and in front of all the guys a cute little bundle of fire and trouble, blondish, more on the petite size, nice figure, nice tight jeans. She's looking like the only one who's got her stuff together.

So she swaggers up to the bar in front of the tender, orders a Manhattan like it was every day. Meanwhile, I lay down a fifty-dollar chip, cover my tab, slide out of the stool. I'm walking past li'l hottie, who's whipping out an ID, bartender's like me, thinking no way these bozos are "of age."

I step out into the world, take a couple steps, then pause to light a smoke, toss the match into the gutter. Shooters' door swings open behind me, and I hear a row. Hottie's yelling, "Danny, you som'bitch! The hell, you said these IDs would be good."

I watch the action from a little ways down from them, unobtrusive. Amused and curious. A morbid fascination with others' problems, I guess.

I guess it's Danny says, with just a twang of whining, "But Janice, I didn't know they'd have an app! The IDs are good, I've used mine a bunch." Hottie starts to lay into him. The two other guys watching how it plays out, probably trying to figure out what the heck they'd do here in the "Biggest Little City in the World" not being able to drink, not being able to gamble. Hell, might as well stand around and watch Hottie tear Danny a new one.

Had just enough drink in me to decide to socialize a bit. I saunter back over to the kids. "So, they got a phone app for IDs now?" taking a drag on my cig, cool like. The couple stops their sidewalk show, and the other two also, all of them wondering what the heck, and I'm seeing the looks on their faces give away their personalities in how they react. Hottie's body language switches from frothing b-word to slinky and sly, with a healthy pinch or two of erotic pheromones. Danny's already had the wind taken outta his sails, so he just sinks deeper in, throwing me a modified stink-eye glare. The other two macho up, stand up straight, shoulders back, then take a step or two back, not really wanting to be on the front line, whatever happens.

Hottie's up for it, bright and glad to tell her story, "Yeah, I saw the app name, Regular or something, Regula?" She takes two steps forward, extends her hand. "I'm Janice. They're Jim and Bob. And this is Danny Boy Dollar." Danny's halfway trying not to lose his cool creds, but having a hard time with it, face set in stone, no expression to speak of. Definite anti-social vibes, if not chronic tendencies in that direction.

I shake her hand, nod all round to the boys. "Well, I'm just a professional gambler, about to shut it down for the night. Or day, now." I smile. I'm told it's a killer smile. Janice—well, you know—smiles with every curve of her body. And Danny's fit to be tied, cinched up good, in some weird position painful and ignoble. But the other two go all juvenile.

"Mister! You're a gambler? Wow, you ever play poker on TV, anything like that? What's the most you've lost?" both Jim and Bob chattering away at once.

"Hold on, guys. One at a time."

Janice says, "Yeah, come on, be cool." They both quiet down.

I try to give Danny an out, hold my hand out to him, say, "Danny Boy Dollar? That's a different name," trying to get him somewhere near comfortable and amused.

I see him argue with his own angel and his own demon, a flash of different tells across his forehead, eyes. He gives in to the inevitable, at least for now, "My dad was a gambler, too. Thought his last name would bring him luck—it didn't. Wound up putting a bullet in his head in some alley around here, broke and broken."

"Sorry to hear that. But, cool name. Dunno why, but it makes me think of Johnny Cash, some rockabilly rock 'n' roller."

"That the guy that did that song, 'Shot a man to watch him die'?"

"That's the one. Song's 'Folsom Prison Blues.' And actually it's: 'Shot a man in Reno, just to watch him die.' Lotta guys think the line 'Turned 21 in prison doing life without parole' was in the same song, but no, that was a Merle Haggard tune, 'Mama Tried.'" Well, maybe "lotta guys" means me, I always got them confused, but no matter, Danny Boy don't give a good or even bad poot anyway.

I turn to the boss of the group, ask Janice, "What you kids gonna do now? Just head back home, wherever that is?"

"Redwood City." The sparkle in her eye is pretty hot, actually. "But I dunno. We drove down here to party 'n' gamble. Anything else to do here?"

Hmm. Take me to the dance, she said. I get an idea. "You kids like to bowl? Probably could get a lane at the biggest, most excessive bowling alley in the world."

Danny Boy practically wrinkles his nose. "Aww, come on. That sounds like kid stuff."

Guy doesn't seem to realize that bowling is right next to shuffleboard, or bocce ball, for old geezer versions of fun. Hot stuff plies her magic on grumpy Dan the Man, sidles up to him, says, "Sounds like fun to me, Danny. You don't want to just drive back home, do ya? We came all this way."

The Jim and Bob show opts in. Bob says, "I'd rather bowl than sit in the car, anyway." Jim nods acquiescence.

Janice turns to me, asks, "How far is it? We need to drive anywhere?"

"Naw, it's about a five-minute walk from here. Let's do it."

Next thing, Dan's again outvoted, we're heading left of Shooters, walking down North Virginia, straight across East 4th. Janice's bopping along, definitely over her fake ID blues. Jim and Bob are lurking back a bit, taking hits off a vape pen. Probably killer smoke, but they aren't offering me any. Guess I'm the old geezer now. But, hey, got my plans. Hottie's primed to be plied with likker is quicker. "Hold up, guys. Be right back," and I leave them on the corner, go down a couple doors on East 4th to Friends Liquor and Convenience, and conveniently pick up a couple pints.

Just takes a couple seconds and I'm back on the corner. Janice is hitting the vape now. Means Danny Boy'll hit the stuff, too, but he's in such a crappy mood he'll probably sink into some sort of horrible funk before the day's out. "Anybody got a safe pocket, hold a mickey?"

Janice exhales her hit and trills, "Ohh! Cool! Here, put one in my purse." Bob's got a jacket on with an inner pocket, he's got number two vodka.

Danny tries to quash the party, "What're we gonna do? Sneak hits in the bowling alley?"

"Got that figured out, Dan. You quote-youngsters-unquote will get nice big sodas. I'll just order beers. We'll look totally legit, except for very discreetly spiking your sodas. It'll be fine."

"Oh." Kid's got some bad mojo up his ass, but then he knows that Janice is getting bored with him; I'd be in the dumps myself.

We head up East 4th on the way to el bowling-o-rama.

8:00 P.M.

Somehow it got to be nighttime. Danny Boy's dissembling behind a buncha shots of vodka and a heavy-duty cannabis vape Bob and Jim keep hunching over, then handing back to Danny. He thinks, *damn, they're gonna get us busted, we'll get kicked out of—oh, what's that sound? Some kinda pipe sound low and then percussion, intricate, loud what the—*"Hey, Danny Boy, you're up!"*—it's that gambler funny he never told us his name, maybe he's some sort of cop or a mafia dude he's all friendly but Janice she won't look my way for hanging all over him I oughta—*

Somehow he's standing at the ball spitty out thing, staring dumbly at the bowling balls, they're slightly jiggling, moving, and Danny hears, "Hey, man, you gonna roll or not?"

"Uh," Danny mumbles, "I'm not sure, maybe I shouldn't..." Voice fades off into the next flicker of a partial scene, like movie film cut up and pasted back together at random, flicker, flicker, flicker— Next he hears, "Ah, man, we're all pretty buzzed, don't worry. Just play the frame."

*Gambler guy is all friendly like My Buddy, but Janice sitting next to him, close, touching he's—*Danny picks a bowling ball up at random, picks it up, two hands, almost throws it over his shoulder—*Dang, Janice's ball, Freudian BS, huh? Ball, balling, old word for the Nasty and what is it a kid's ball? Like five pounds or something*—drops the ball from about six inches up, thuds into the track with the rest of the balls, he picks another one—*this one feels heavy, thumb hole is huge, sweaty—Janice's leaving me we're through, short time but she's so sexy and*—Danny addresses the lane, steps forward, ball backswing, sweaty thumb hole, up to the line, throwing the ball, slips out of his grip, arcs up in the air, crashes down on the boards with a bang, bounces twice, drops into the right gutter, putters on down the lane...

Somehow, gets through the second throw, back to his seat next to Jim and Bob, Janice to his right, but slid over next to that guy—*this is like stupid, why'm I here, it's too noisy in here, with that music, the low pipe and sharp percussion, so intricate but I'm wanting out of here OH! it's not music it's a bowling alley, buncha people here now, balls rolling down the alley, smacking into pins, it's not music, bowling alleys aren't music I must be crazy, hell, I gotta get outta here somebody gonna see me, I look crazy, I feel crazy*—then flicker—*hell, I'm walking, walking past the guy at the counter he knows, knows I'm like, stoned, big time, knows I'm crazy*—flicker—walking towards the glass door out—*it's—what're all those patterns and lights oh—oh never mind, just reflections in the glass and*—whoosh! through the doors—*like a birth, an opening up out in the night air feels good but—Janice—hell*—flicker, and some body-memory takes him to the right on the sidewalk, down to the end of the block, turns, waiting for the light to change to cross the street—*the color's supposed to be...red to walk? But it's red, and I'm not walking, must be the other color when will it change wait there's words, say "don't walk" ok so I'm—oh crap it changed now it says "walk" and it's, yeah, green*—flicker—*the hell, how'm I here, cross the street, a couple doors down and the neighborhood, it's a creepy little neighborhood, broke down, expect there to be drunks, junkies shuffling around, gambling burnouts like my Dad*—flicker.

Flicker flicker flicker and body memory takes him back to the car—*burned in my brain, always remember where you park, park what? car, car is... is... second floor*—pulls it up from a deep part of his brain—*orange section, different colors for different sections, colors on the posts parked right next to one on the far side there*—flicker—he unlocks the car, chir-rup, goes to the passenger side—*somebody's gonna come, see me getting in the car—wait it's my car I can get in it ok, but I'm crazy, must be I keep hearing noises an' voices and*—flicker—sitting in the passenger seat, glove box open, reaching in—*gun. Dad's .38 Special he was always afraid, loan sharks, or thieves, taking his winnings, 'cept he never won, just more and more lost until bam! this gun, ended it but this gun, I need it now*—flicker—

Back on the sidewalk, not much traffic out, quiet Tuesday night, gun tucked back of his jeans, flannel shirt covering it up—flicker—*Oh yeah, the guy, he went straight across the street to get the hooch, maybe that's what I need*—flicker—*what'm I doing here? oh liquor, what do I want, wait do I have money*—standing in front of the counter, at the cash register, little oriental guy's waiting for him to make up his mind, sees him reach around to back pocket for wallet and—flicker—*this little weenie doing all wild eye and hands coming up he looks afraid wait he knows I'm crazy wait why's he look afraid*—Danny looks down at his hand, pointing the pistol at the clerk, back up to the clerk—*oh crap what'm I doing? Am I robbing the place? No, only a crazy person'd do that oh crap oh bigger crap*—Danny mumbles, quiet, "Oh, sorry, I thought you were somebody else," lowers the gun, pointing down to the floor now—*oh yeah, that makes sense, thought you were somebody else, the OTHER liquor store guy that I really DID mean to take aim at oh crap oh bigger crap he's gonna call the cops I gotta*—flicker—

On the street now, walking fast, real fast, but not running, heading back to the bowling alley—*no not alley, bowling stadium, king of all bowling alleys, with that sound, echo-y, droning wuh- wuh- wuh- wuh- WHAM! ka-bam-a-tinkle-slam but Janice oh that guy, he's probably in her panties now, got her all wet and*—flicker—whoosh through the doors into the mael-strom—*that noise and now a chittering high-pitched background sound oh it's people, laughing and talking and*—flicker— coming back to the game, somebody's talking: "Hey, there's Danny! The hell you been, man! We been worried about you," Bob's saying, Janice and gambler dude trying to look all concerned but with a shadowy edge—*perhaps guilt, maybe getting caught a little too close together, huh?*

9:15 P.M.

I could see Danny Boy was bad off. I mean, he was loaded enough when he left, but now... completely dysfunctional, and looking like in a state of shock or something, pale, shaking, eyes darting between the four of us, mouthing words but no sound coming out.

Janice says, "Danny, hey, it's ok. Where'd you go?"

Jim calls out, practically screeching, "He's got a gun!"

Sure enough, he's holding a snub-nosed revolver at his side, the only calm normal gesture, everybody's carrying a phone or some dumb crap or other, just stuff in people's hands all the time, but yeah, a gun.

Danny starts, looks down at his hand holding the pistol, gasps like it came from nowhere and appeared there. His eyes narrow then, he looks up at Janice, then over to me. He grins, a horrible grimace. He finally gets some words out, says to me, "The hell you doing? Janice's mine!" Like he had the title and registration on the cute little hottie and I was a thief broke into his house at night.

And, like I was a thief in the night in his house, the gun comes up, pointed at me.

I see a bit of commotion over his shoulder, way over at the desk. A security guard and two cops, conferring with the dull-eyed attendant at the desk, the attendant pointing our way. Looks like Danny Boy didn't go unnoticed after all, either he did something while he was away or someone noticed the pistol. The cops look our way.

I say to Danny, "Don't do it, man. Remember the song. You don't want that, do you?"

"You! I don't care what you say!" The pistol, his hand shaking with rage, wavers in front of me, as close enough to point blank to make it a sure shot should he pull the trigger.

Janice says, "No! There's cops, look, they're coming here!" Danny glances over his shoulder, sees them rushing over our way, unstrapping their sidearms or whatever, turns back to me, a fire in his eyes.

He lowers the pistol a bit, says to Janice, "You made me do this! I'd kill him for you, to keep what we have alive, but yeah, I don't wanna 'turn 21 in prison.' Hell with it..."

He turns to me. "I want to watch you die. But I'm not going to be 21 in prison." Then the pistol goes to his temple and as the cops get close to us he splatters his brains to bits in front of all of us.

10:15 A.M. Several weeks later

That's what happens when people let their problems get to them.

Now, it's Tuesday again.

Me, no problems.

There were lots of questions from a lot of cops and such, but bottom line, there were a crap-ton of witnesses to the fact that Danny Boy Dollar did himself in after pointlessly threatening some poor clerk a couple blocks away, all with no help from anyone else. By dawn they'd done with Jim, Bob, Janice, and myself. I'd asked Janice if she had to get back to Danny's family or whatever, make arrangements, but she declined.

What it came down to, the Jim and Bob show somehow stumbled back to their cave somewhere, and Janice and I shacked up for a while, a couple weeks or so. One thing about spending a lot of time and money in a casino, it's basically no cost for them to comp an otherwise vacant room, figuring it'll come out in their favor eventually, and it always does. But that's another problem I don't have.

So, she and I hung out in my room, did a few things, spent time in bed, got to see her naked. Figured that Danny really did get tail off a tiger, she's pretty and sexy and knows it, and he was in way over his head, never saw it coming.

Me, I knew what was coming. I knew when she didn't bat an eye when I came on to her, subtle though I was. And I knew that she'd get bored quick. It turned weird fast, petty BS, lots of time with no talk, yadda-yadda. She moved on, don't know where, don't care. She's trading in on her erotic charm, and me, I'm cool as a cucumber on ice.

See? No problem.

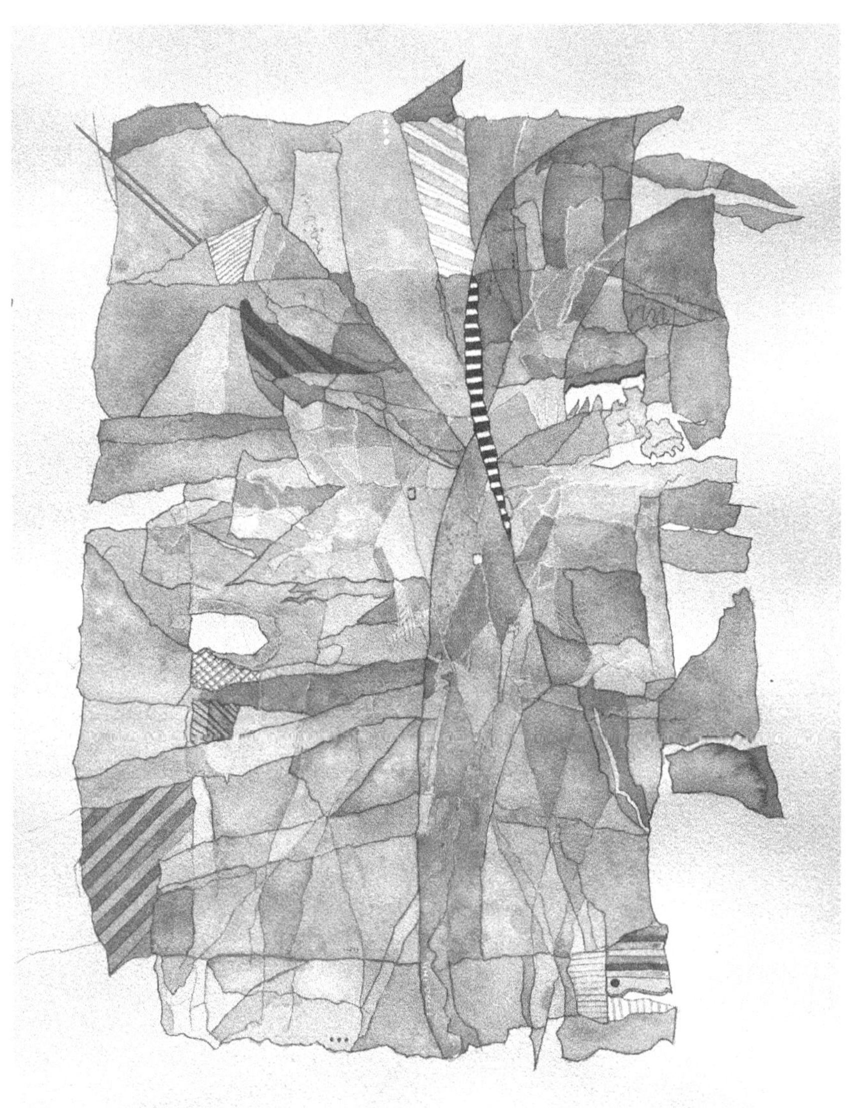

Hundred Acre Wood #5: Rabbit Has a Birthday Party by Kim Smith, watercolor and ink, 2023

Shugacitay

(Ode to C & H Sugar Factory, Crockett, California)
by Kathleen Hermann

30,000 tons
Boat from Brazil
Belly so heavy
She rides low
Under the bridge
Up to the dock
Dwarfed by metropolis
Of steel brick and glass
Called Shugacitay

Cranes dig deep
Into the hold
Building crystal mountains
Of raw gold
Melt it
Spin it
Purify and dry
Pink and white boxes
Stockpiled high

Four million pounds
Pour from the gates
On trucks and on trains
To thirteen states

Old brick factory
Clean new tech
Engineered to refine and protect
Steampunk ironworks stained aqua and rust
Exhale mighty cumulous puffs
Blinking marquee flashes LEDs
'Til apricot dawn breaks upon Shugacitay
Shoo shoo sweet Shugacitay

Ray's Abalone Dinner

by Deborah Morrison

Brushing the dirt off my hands and slipping off my muddy garden boots, I grabbed the large brass doorknob and pushed. The warmth and noise engulfed me as I closed the door behind me with a shove. Gone was the quiet, the soft background rush of waves, the cool misty air that landed gently on my face and clothes, staying there as tiny droplet companions until I brushed them off.

Standing still and unnoticed at the entry, I paused. The smell of melting butter wafted through the crowd and hit my nose. The kitchen was to the left of me around the massive stone fireplace. It, like the garden I had just left, were my places of refuge. These large groups of weekend/week-long visitors always exhausted me. I followed the scent of butter, smiling but not engaging, as I stepped carefully through and around the sprawling clumps of people scattered all over the room, heads together, talking in deep concentration.

Butter and olive oil sizzled in the large frying pan. Stirring the butter until it melted, my father-in-law hummed softly in a world of his own. Turning, he took the filleted pieces of abalone, spread each one flat on the chopping board, and proceeded to pound the milky pink flesh until it was translucent. His beard and hair whipped back and forth as his wooden mallet connected with the flesh. Beads of perspiration grew on his forehead and he absent-mindedly wiped his hand across to brush them aside. A glass of ruby colored wine sat next to him on the counter. He took a sip and continued his pounding.

I stood watching, unnoticed, as he worked alone in the kitchen, preparing a meal for the crowd that filled the house. Gales of laughter and loud voices raised in conversations that were borderline arguments drowned out his quiet humming.

The meaning of life, the relationship of women to society, tarot, the unconscious, the subconscious, Jungian psychology, dream analysis, all were being tossed around and over the big oak table next to the kitchen. These were the topics my mother-in-law was fascinated with. She drew people from all over the world, who came willingly to partake of her open-door policy and beautiful surroundings. Food was always included. She loved the energy, the lively talk, and she blossomed under the adoration. The tasks of life, like feeding people, were afterthoughts, typically handled by family members.

Random people came and went during these week-long gatherings. Some sitting down to talk for hours, others moving from room to room, jumping in and out of the throng, some just passing through the conversations to wander outside to explore the bluffs and tide pools below the house. Many minds, many voices, much wine, and overall good cheer filled the dining room, which was only separated from the kitchen by the huge chopping board countertop where Ray worked. He seemed as oblivious to them as these guests were to him. Not a single person seemed to take any interest at all in what he was doing, let alone offer to help. On and on and on the energetic talk continued, with arms flailing in emphasis.

I skirted the weekend visitors and made my way to him, as I was bored with all the endless talking. It was day two of hosting my mother-in-law's friends.

"Need any help, Ray? I asked.

"Sure, thanks," he said, pointing me towards a paper bag lying on the counter and pouring me a glass of wine. I took a sip. It was delicious. Ray knew his wine, that's for sure, I thought.

"Pour some flour with a dash of salt and pepper into that bag." I gathered the things and shook the flour around in the bag.

"Toss some of these pieces in." I did so, and he took the bag from me, forked them out, piece by piece, placing each one gently in the melted butter and oil. The smell began to fill the room with its loveliness. The small pieces sizzled their lively dance in the pan, the edges curling a bit and becoming a beautiful golden brown. He flipped each one quickly, after just a minute or two, and placed them carefully on plates lined with paper towels.

"These are the two abalone I caught on my last dive. They were hard to find," he said quietly, as he continued his filleting and pounding. I shook the pounded pieces in the bag of flour, then handed the bag back to him to drop the pieces into the pan. The beautiful mother-of-pearl shells sat empty of their flesh on the countertop, the blues and greens glowing against the rough, drab, gray outer shell. This hard-won delicacy made it to the table only after hours of diving. Underwater, Ray had pried the bumpy, gray barnacle-covered shells off of the rocky cliff bottoms that surrounded the house, braving huge waves and the powerful tide. He managed to make his quota this last dive (two full-grown abalone), but he wasn't always lucky, and many dives he came home empty-handed.

"Do you think there will be enough?" I asked as I glanced around and did a mental headcount of the crowd at the table, the other group in the living room, as well as the guests who had walked down to Russian Gulch and would be showing up hungry any minute.

"Looks like we'll have about 30 people or so," I said worriedly. Ray did a quick lift of one of his bushy eyebrows, then quietly pointed to the meat he was filleting and pounding.

"Don't worry, I'm ahead of you. This batch is really chicken, and I have lots of that," he said in a quiet voice as he gave me a quick wink.

I looked at him, seeing a side of Ray I had never seen before.

"What?" I leaned in and whispered in his ear. "Really? Won't they know?"

"Of course not, don't worry. They'll never notice," he whispered back as he clinked my glass, took a sip of the rich red wine, and smiled conspiratorially.

"What's for dinner?" one of the guests called out towards the kitchen.

Ray and I looked at each other, smiled, and, without a moment's hesitation, said in unison, "Abalone."

Enjoying a Bagel

by Louise Moises

Bagel, the pit bull-boxer mix, strains at the leash.
David, his master, wears a pouch of doggie treats.
A block away, I hear him say, *Sit, Bagel, Sit,*
his voice stern and serious. He pushes the dog's butt
into a sitting position, and hands over a treat.

The pair advances towards me. Bagel's long tail
can be seen whipping from side to side,
and I am grateful that he hasn't been lopped,
like some of his breed.

I stop my weeding, address the dog by name.
Happy to see me, Bagel rises from the sidewalk,
all fours in the air, executes a mid-air wiggle,
touching his nose to his hip, tail wildly wagging.

My laughter further excites his canine versatility.
Now he dances on his hind legs, front paws
repeatedly hitting the pavement. David pulls,
ineffectively on the leash. *Sit, Bagel, Sit.*

Bagel's slick black and white coat catches
the morning light, shines like a domino.
Perhaps, a better name than Bagel or maybe
Oreo. But what do I know?

A slight loosening of the leash,
and Bagel's big front paws land on my chest,
his tongue swipes my face from ear to ear,
his breath smells of damp old chew toys.

I can't resist the jibe, *So how's the training
going, David?* Now all three of us are laughing,
Bagel's lips rolled back in a grin. I laugh so hard,
I cry. Finally, David checks his phone,

drags Bagel down the sidewalk.
As they round the corner, Bagel looks back
at me, with what I like to think of as longing.
See you tomorrow, Bagel, I call out.

The last of his tail waves like a flag,
as they round the corner.
I resume my weeding surrounded
by an aura of joy.

Poets and Prose Writers

Peter Bray is a graduate of UC Berkeley and a Benicia resident since 1983. He's written and published three chapbooks and has 16 original songs on YouTube.com. He's written a column, "The A Cappella Handyman—The Poetry Guy," for the *Benicia Herald* since 2008 and won the Benicia Love Poetry Contest that same year. He's a member of Benicia's First Tuesday Poets and Benicia Literary Arts. His creative newsletter, "Taproot & Aniseweed—The Naked Oyster," has been in nearly continuous publication since 1987.

Suzanne Bruce holds a B.S. in Education from the University of Tulsa and did graduate work in Behavior Disorders at Wichita State University. Suzanne has been the emcee for the *Solano County Library Foundation's Authors Luncheon* for six years. In 2022, she conducted an on-stage conversation with author Amy Tan. Her poems have won several prizes, and have been published in numerous journals, such as *Copperfield Review*, *Phati'tude*, and *Interlitq*. Her books, *Voices Beyond the Canvas* (2007)  and *Her Visions Her Voices* (2015), are ekphrastic duets with artist Janet Manalo (www.ekphrasticexpressions.com). She is the current Poet Laureate of Fairfield.

Johanna Ely is the author of four poetry books: *Transformation, Tides of the Heart—Poems for Benicia, Postcards From a Dream* (Blue Light Press, 2020*)*, and *What Still Matters* (Last Laugh Productions, 2023). She is an award-winning poet who has been published in literary journals and anthologies, including *California Quarterly* and *The Poeming Pigeon*. She has been nominated for a Pushcart Prize, and was the 2022 winner of the Benicia Love Poetry Contest. Johanna served as the sixth poet laureate of Benicia, California, and is a board member of the Ina Coolbrith Circle of Poets, one of the oldest poetry groups in California.

Tamar Enoch is now fully retired from her careers as a molecular biologist, speech therapist, bookkeeper, and non-profit administrator. She credits the Benicia Literary Arts Memoir Group she has been part of for more than seven years for giving  her the inspiration and discipline to write regularly and to explore different literary forms. She is especially grateful to Upaya Zen Center for offering an online Haiku workshop in the winter of 2021 during the depths of the COVID lockdown. Haiku gave so many of us, around the world, a vehicle to express our hopes, fears and humor during that dark time of isolation. Tamar is a dedicated mindfulness and meditation practitioner. When she isn't writing, she enjoys playing ping-pong or strumming her ukulele.

 In the 1960s, **Stacy Gardner**'s mom gave her a copy of *Harriett the Spy*, and Stacy has wanted to write books (and spy) ever since. When she wasn't reading and spying, Stacy created art and decided her second career would be as an artist living in a Parisian garret or as a Go-Go dancer on Laugh-In. Sticking as close to her plan as possible, Stacy moved from Sacramento to the Bay Area, owned tons of art supplies, but made very little art. She still loves to read and spy, and she plans to write a book before she dies.

Mary Susan Gast is a poet, writer, theologian, and human rights advocate. She lived her first 17 years on a small farm outside the tiny town of Baroda, Michigan, then took off to places and adventures unforeseen by anyone, and unimagined by her. She is dazzled in retrospect by all the odd turns her life has taken, and by the generous people who have cared for her along the way. Her newspaper column, "Going the Distance," began during the pandemic and continues, drawing together a community of mutual support. Mary Susan served as Benicia's eighth Poet Laureate.

Beth Grimm is a local Benician involved actively in literary and creative arts. She says she's not a poet, but when the mood strikes her and she's looking for a way to express emotions in the fewest words possible, she turns to poetry. She spends the rest of her time writing prose, mainly nonfiction, memoir and family stories, and little books that inspire creativity. Her most recently published written works appear in Benicia Literary Arts anthologies, a column in the *Benicia Herald* called "The Benicia Walker," Mary Susan Gast's "Going the Distance" *Benicia Herald* column, and her published book, *The Great Grandpa Chronicles*. She's also active in the Arts community, and her art and books can be seen at The Little Art Shop and The Depot in Benicia.

Evie Groch, Ed.D., is a Field Supervisor/ Mentor for new administrators in Graduate Schools of Education. Her opinion pieces, humor, poems, short stories, recipes, word challenges, and other articles have been widely published in the *New York Times*, the *San Francisco Chronicle*, the *East Bay Times*, *The Journal*, *Games Magazine*, and many online venues. Many of her poems are in published anthologies. Her travelogues have been published online with Grand Circle Travel. The themes of travel, language, immigration, and justice are special for her, and she focuses on them in her poetry book, *Half the Hurricanes*. Evie serves as the current president of the Ina Coolbrith Circle of poets, established in 1919.

An educator for over 30 years, **Nancy Haskett** retired in 2011 and is a member of the Ina Coolbrith Circle, MoSt (Modesto Stanislaus Poetry Center), as well as a small, local writing group. Her work has appeared in more than 40 publications, including the anthology *More than Soil, More than Sky*; Stanislaus *Connections*; *Homestead Review*; *Iodine Press*; *Song of the San Joaquin*; *The Pen Woman*; *Monterey Poetry Review*; *Penumbra*; and more. In her spare time, Nancy enjoys reading, traveling, walking, and spending time with her family. Her poetry collection, *Shadows & Reflections*, is available on Amazon.

Linda Hastings is retired from a career in corporate executive management with a focus on developmental training, cultural creation, performance measurement, and conflict resolution. Linda's diverse life experiences and challenges have provided the opportunity for inner awareness and a quest for the truth that is possible through an open heart. A deep dive into memoir writing has opened a window into understanding and compassion for herself and for all those struggling to brighten our world. A resident of the Bay Area since 1971, Linda currently lives in Benicia and volunteers for Benicia Literary Arts and the Tim & Jeannie Hamann Foundation. She is also a contributing columnist for Benicia Magazine.

Kathleen Herrmann writes poems inspired by small moments which carry big messages. Her poems have appeared in anthologies published by B Cubed Press, Ice Floe Press, Pure Slush, Moonstone Press, Napa Valley Writers, and Benicia Literary Arts. She has also been published in the "Going the Distance" column in the *Benicia Herald*. She was awarded Best in Show at the Solano County Fair in 2022 and 2023. She hosts literary interviews on OZCAT radio and is writing a poetry book about refugees to America, entitled *I Was There, Now I'm Here.*

Rick Hocker, a fourteen-year resident of Martinez, is the author of *Four in the Garden*, an award-winning spiritual allegory about trusting in God. His book is a reimagining of the Garden of Eden story, except that the Creator doesn't make a human companion for the first human, but offers an intimate relationship with himself instead. Rick has been part of a Martinez writing group for thirteen years. He wrote monthly inspirational articles for the *Martinez Tribune* faith section. He is a game programmer by day. In his free time, he is finishing his second novel, a mystery thriller. Website: www.rickhocker.com.

Sandy King was born and raised in the San Francisco Bay Area too many years ago to remember. She has always loved the outdoors. Now retired, she spends her time in her garden, hiking in the Sierra Nevada Mountains, spoiling her two beloved Dalmatians, and writing poetry and short stories. Her writing is most often about the wonders of nature, especially the animals. Many of her poems have been published in *The Avocet Journal*, as well as in local poetry publications.

Born and raised in Minnesota, **Ramona Lappier** is a poet, who, via Hawaii and Washington, has lived for nearly 40 years in northern California. Her poetry has appeared in the Benicia Literary Arts publications *Nooks and Crannies* (the Benicia First  Tuesday Poets' eighth Anthology) and *Yearning to Breathe Free—A Community Journal of 2020*, as collected from the *Benicia Herald* column, "Going the Distance." Her recorded poems have aired on Vallejo radio station 89.5 KZCT/Ozcat Radio. Ramona is the mom of two sons and the "Grandma Monie" of three grandchildren.

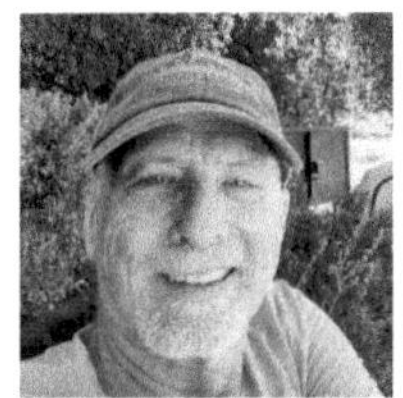 Throughout his life, **Michael MacDonald** has been drawn to a series of creative outlets—most consistently creative writing, but including photography and digital graphics manipulation, music and sound. While serving on the Board of Directors for the Benicia Theatre Group and volunteering in back-and-front-of-stage support, his day job revolves around software support. Living in Benicia with his wife and children, he says, "I thank the Carquinez Review for publishing one of my stories, and I look forward to being able to continue to contribute to the Carquinez/Solano literary milieu."

Karen Marker is an Oakland-based poet and memoirist whose work draws on her family roots and branches in places that include Muir Beach, New Orleans, Sweden, New England, Ohio, and Vilna. She also  turns to her studies of psychology, classical mythology, and religion for inspiration. Her work has recently been published in *The MacGuffin*, has won awards through the Ina Coolbrith Circle and the Soul-Making Keats Literary Competition, and has been included in the Kent

State University May 4th Archives, as well as a number of anthologies. Her chapbook with Finishing Line Press will be coming out in the next year.

Louise Moises, a graduate of San Jose State, was born and raised in the Bay Area, where she still resides. She has been a teacher, storyteller, puppeteer, and the owner of an antiquarian bookstore. She started writing poetry in 2017 as a means of dealing with grief, but her vision has since expanded to include a wide range of subjects. Her poems have been recognized by the Ina Coolbrith Circle and Artist Embassy International, among others. She has been published in numerous anthologies. Her first chapbook will be available in the Spring from Finishing Line Press. Louise says: "I am very grateful for the poetry community that has welcomed me with open arms."

Deborah Morrison has used pen and paper all her life to write about the people and places she loves. When she isn't writing or spending time with her family and friends, you can find her in her garden carefully tending monarch butterflies, chickens, bees, a dog, a cat, and assorted other wonderful creatures that make their way into her life.

Rob Rogers is a writer, teacher and journalist who works with 11th- and 12th-grade students at De La Salle High School in Concord and lives in Vallejo, California. "When I'm not nattering on about transcendentalism, the American Dream, or my cats, you can find me puttering in the garden, learning to play harmonica, or playing Minecraft with my ten- and thirteen-year-old sons. "I grew up in Plymouth, Massachusetts, attended Kenyon

College, and spent several years as a newspaper reporter and travel writer before finding my home in the classroom. I am a strong believer in the power of stories, the need for creative self-expression, and the 12-bar blues. I also like coffee."

Jane Russell lives in Pittsburg, California, with her two beautiful cats and partner Petey. She is a retired teacher, school counselor, college instructor and Marriage Family Therapist (MFT). Being a longtime Sierra Club member and avid traveler, she especially  enjoys writing poems about places she has visited and her experiences with nature and the environment. She belongs to two creative writing critique circles and is a member of the San Francisco Bay Area Ina Coolbrith Poetry Circle. Some of her poems have been published in *The Avocet—A Journal of Nature Poetry*, the *Suisun Valley Review* (Spring, 2023), and *Vistas and Byways Review* (SF State OLLI, Fall 2023). Besides writing poetry, she also enjoys music, especially folk music. She plays the guitar and mountain dulcimer and sings with the Diablo Valley Threshold Singers, an *a capella* women's singing group.

 **Alyza Lee Salomon** has worked as a tutor, editor, and educator. She ascribes her love of words and languages to a trilingual childhood, growing up as a first-generation American. Her poems have appeared in local anthologies. As a dancer, she has performed with Natica Angilly's Poetic Dance Theater Company since 2003. Alyza studied at Harpur College (now Binghamton U) and earned her master's degree in English Literature at Sonoma State University. She grew up on the East Coast and now enjoys the natural wonders and cultural diversity of living in the SF Bay Area.

Deborah Bachels Schmidt has self-published four chapbooks, with a fifth, *Stumbling into Grace,* published by Orchard Street Press. With Mary Eichbauer, Johanna Ely, and Laurie Hailey, she is co-author of *Love's Meditation*  (Random Lane Press, 2023). Her poems have appeared in journals, including *Blue Unicorn, California Quarterly, The Ekphrastic Review, The Lyric,* and *The MacGuffin,* as well as in anthologies such as *Pandemic Puzzle Poems, From Pandemic to Protest,* and *Upside Down and From Below.* A Pushcart nominee, she has earned awards from the Poets' Dinner, the Coolbrith Circle, the Soul-Making Keats Literary Competition, and Orchard Street Press.

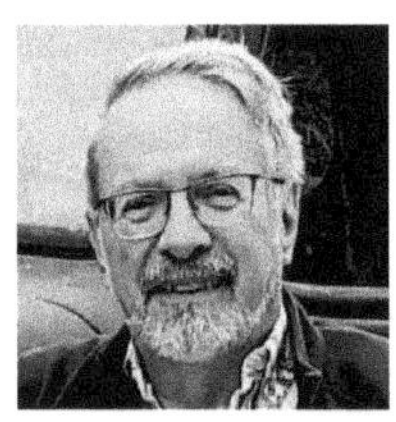

Woodrow Shiftlett, known as Woody, sometimes calls himself "the unlikely poet." With a BS and PhD in chemical engineering and an MBA, just what is he doing writing poetry after a lifetime of technical and business writing? Simple, Woody started writing poetry some 50-plus years ago, gave it up for a busy career, and now returns with the loving encouragement of his much more poetically talented partner. He loves to write about life experiences and historical themes. Woody enjoys hiking, particularly along the Carquinez Strait, bicycling, kayaking, and skiing, all of which inspire his writing.

Sandra D. Simmer loves living her retirement years on a marina in the Bay Area near her children and new grandchildren. She enjoys activities such as writing, painting, traveling, and socializing with family and friends. Sandra has short stories, memoirs,  and poems published in various anthologies. Her first novel, *The Reclamation: Earth Under Siege,* was published on

Amazon in January 2023. Visit her website at https://www.sandradsimmer.com for updates on her creative work and activities.

Thomas Eric Stanton is primarily known as a California Surrealist. His works engage many media and often emphasize the aspects of "Performance." He has produced books of poetry and his paintings are included in many public, private, and museum collections. He lives and works in Benicia, California. He served as the eighth Poet Laureate of Benicia, California, from 2018 to 2020.

Nancy Tolin is a California artist and writer of poetry and prose. She works in a variety of media, including painting, drawing, printmaking, assemblage, and advertising design. She holds a bachelor's degree in studio art from the University of California at Davis. Her visual work has been shown in national-juried shows. Her recent poetry has been published in local newspaper columns and anthologies. Often, at 3:00 am, she searches for her mischievous Muse, who delights in playing hide-and-seek games in her mind.

Jonathan Watson, Texas-born but California-raised, is a law librarian and poet in Northern California. He received his B.A. in English from UC Berkeley, M.A. in English from CSU Sacramento, and MLIS from San Jose State University. (He and his mother, Jo-Ann Watson, graduated together). His poetry often addresses themes of family, identity, and heritage, with his mother often acting as a muse. His poem, "Nomad," was featured in *Avatar Review* (Summer 2006, Issue 8). He enjoys reading at local poetry events and conducting historical research.

Gail Wasserman is a poet/lyricist from Benicia who serves on the Benicia Literary Arts Board and has ten publications in the "Going the Distance, Not There Yet" column of the *Benicia Herald*, several publications with Moonstone Arts Press, and a publication in the American Graveyard Anthology of "Read and Green Books." In addition, Gail has received Honorable Mention in the Ina Coolbrith 2022 and 2023 contests. When Gail is not writing poetry or lyrics, she is practicing Family Law in Contra Costa and San Diego Counties.

Rooted in Oakland, California, **Linda Wright** graduated from UC Berkeley in Psychology, with an emphasis in child development. Wright worked as a group facilitator for Cru International at Ohio State, Cornell, and Howard University, teaching Christian leadership skills to college students. Next she taught parenting skills to pregnant women who were in a drug rehabilitation center at Mandela House in Oakland. For the last nineteen years, she focused on teaching social and emotional skills to children from kindergarten to fifth grade, and then she retired. Wright earned a storytelling certificate from Stagebridge Senior Art Center and has mesmerized audiences at various Bay Area venues and elementary schools. Wright's passion is to make history come alive to audiences from preschoolers to seniors, on the stage and in print. Wright is a member of Faithful Central Bible Church, West Coast Christian Writers, Storytelling Association of California, Benicia Literary Arts, Society of Children's Book Writers and Illustrators, and the National Storytelling Network. Wright is also a member of the advisory committee for the Chico State Valene Smith Museum of Anthropology. She is married to Randy Wright and they have three children.

Artists

Steve Barbaria's art practice combines current events, historical reference, a love of nature, and concern for social justice. "My early career as a political cartoonist and editorial illustrator connected me to stories that shape our society. On assignment, I interpreted news events, book reviews and cultural stories, developing visual narratives for regional and national publications. As a creative director for 30+ years, composition, visual hierarchy, form, and color were an integral part of my work. These experiences provide through-lines to my painting practice today."

Annette Laurel Batchelor writes: "Many places have brought me great joy and memories of personal exploration of beaches, hikes in forests, exploring landscapes, cityscapes, flora, and wildlife. I spend hours carefully creating and painting compositions of expressive images out in nature, Plein air, and in the studio. My paintings tend to lean towards a painterly fashion with an impressionistic flair. I love creating pieces that draw attention and imagination to tell a story. I have been honored to show my work in local, national, and international juried shows, earning several reward recognitions to boot! My greatest reward, of course, is when others find pleasure in my work. It's most gratifying when someone appreciates my art enough to want to place it in their home.

Diana Krevsky is a longtime resident of Vallejo and has been making art at her Hunters Point Shipyard studio for an even longer time. Varied in approach and art media, her political and social commentary works have been widely exhibited throughout California and beyond. Active within the Bay Area arts community and involved with environmental issues locally, she continues her art journey to this day, reflecting personal views about cultural identity, values of society and its body politic. Often, irony, humor and whimsy act as conduits for materializing those ideas, in addition to expressing the physical and emotional world as observed.

Lori Larks was raised in the San Francisco Bay Area and received her Bachelor of Science Degree in Conservation at the University of California, Berkeley. During summers as a teen and college student, she worked as a small-craft instructor and river guide. While a student at Berkeley, she took studio painting courses from invited European painters as well as courses in typography and old-style printing. She was hired as a typesetter/typographer for local print shops, supporting herself through graduate school, pursuing a master's degree that then led to a career in public service. During that time, raising her son, she also coached soccer for over a decade and served as a sports photographer for a local gymnastics club. Her love of the natural environment and being outside, combined with her love of art, led her to painting plein air. Her work, both paintings and photography, are exhibited in local galleries.

Jennifer Lothrigel is a photographer, writer and artist in the San Francisco Bay area (East Bay.) Her work is inspired by nature, the body, healing, memory, and mysticism. Jennifer's work has been exhibited nationally in galleries and museums and is held in private collections. She is the author of *Pneuma* (Liquid Light Press, 2018), *Wormhole Weaver* (self-published, 2022), and *Secret Futures* (Bottlecap Press, 2023). Find her on Instagram @ JenniferLothrigel.

R. Kim Smith was born in New York, New York. She received a BFA in Studio Arts from Syracuse University, continuing her studies post-graduate from Syracuse University, Arizona State University, and College of Marin. She worked for over 30 years in the film industry in Visual Effects and is now retired from that industry. She has shown internationally, including a solo show at Green Collections Multiple in Tokyo, Japan. Among other recent shows she was included in the de Young Open 2023, the Mercury 20 Gallery group show "Metamorphosis," and the Crocker Kingsley Annual 2022–2023. She resides in Benicia.

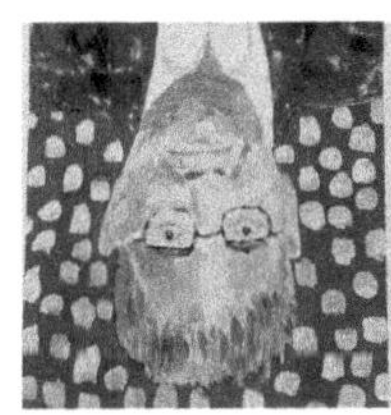

Morrie Warshawski is a retired strategic planning consultant. Before becoming a consultant, he was the Executive Director of three nonprofit arts organizations, including Bay Area Video Coalition in San Francisco. His works as an artist and poet have appeared in galleries and publications internationally. He makes his home in Napa, CA, where he can be found painting, drawing, writing and growing tomatoes.

Claudia Waters is a contemporary figurative painter who works in oil on fine linen. Her paintings have been shown extensively in national and regional exhibitions, including the Katonah Museum of Art, Islip Art Museum, Hunterdon Art Museum, Trenton

City Museum at Ellarslie, Arnot Art Museum, Butler Institute of American Art, City Without Walls, Johnson & Johnson, The Monmouth Museum, MarinMOCA, Arc Gallery SF, Marin Society of Artists, and Arts Benicia. A solo exhibition, "A Deeper Dive," of her figurative pool paintings was held at Novato Gallery in 2022. Her painting "Big Merge/Submerge"

was featured on the official Tumblr of the San Francisco Museum of Modern Art, Submission Friday, in 2019. She received the Hunterdon Art Museum Prize for her painting "Shoreward Gaze" in 2017. She earned her BFA from the Parsons School of Design and also studied painting at the Yard School of Art and printmaking at the Art Students League. She lives and works in the San Francisco Bay Area.

Kenneth Weichel lives in Benicia, California. He has received a bachelor's and a master's degree from San Francisco State University. In 1976 he started Androgyne Books, a small independent press. For ten years, he edited and published a literary journal, *Androgyne*. Since 1980, Androgyne Books has published twenty books, including poetry, fiction, biography, translations, and essays. Ken's poetry, prose, and collages have appeared in many literary magazines and online journals. He has published two books of short fiction and two books of poetry, as well as a collage poem, "Horse Drawn." Currently he is working on collages and other book projects.

Sabina Yates graduated with a four-year diploma from the Art Institute of Chicago. Later she got her BFA from Sonoma State University. She taught Painting and Drawing at the Santa Rosa Junior College for 37 years. She has exhibited widely in juried shows and galleries through the years and has had several one-woman shows. "As a student at the Art Institute of Chicago, I walked past masterpieces every day as I went to my classes. As a teacher at Santa Rosa Junior College, I tried to incorporate the history of painting and drawing into my teaching. After retiring and moving to Benicia, I realized that 'theory had outstripped practice,' and I have tried to work through many of the ideas and theories of art that have obsessed painters throughout history."

About Benicia Literary Arts

Benicia Literary Arts is a 501(c)3 nonprofit organization that serves our community by holding events and presentations of interest to writers and readers, and by publishing works of fiction, non-fiction, and poetry. We hold panel discussions, poetry and prose readings, workshops on writing technique and self-promotion, and receptions where readers and writers gather to mingle and converse. We sponsor writing critique groups where authors share their work and exchange ideas.

A sample of our publications:

Carquinez Review 2020

Nooks and Crannies, a First Tuesday Poets Anthology
    (ed. Thomas Stanton)

Joel Fallon (ed. Don Peery and Mary Eichbauer)—*The Book of Joel* (honored by Artists Embassy International)

Yearning to Breathe Free: A Community Journal of 2020
    (ed. Mary Susan Gast and Mary Eichbauer)

Carolyn Plath—*Glenn's Sister, A Memoir* (Finalist, 2023 Next Generation Indie Book Awards)

Lois Requist—*Late Harvest Green*
    (Finalist, 2019 Next Generation Indie Book Awards)

Donnell Rubay—*With a Dream So Proud, The Life of Stephen Vincent Benet*

Joan Gefland—*The Long Blue Room* (poetry)

June Oxford—*The Capital That Couldn't Stay Put*

Visit our website at www.benicialiteraryarts.org for more information or to get involved.

Notes About the Type

Dejanire, used throughout this book, was released in 2019. It is a type family loosely inspired by an anonymous display typeface found in a type specimen by Claude Lamesle, published in Paris in 1742. Ramiro Espinoza is the type designer, based in The Hague. Dejanire is a transitional roman with a marked contrast and a crisp presence in print

The Hague, the capital city of the South Holland province of the Netherlands, is known as the international city of peace and justice. For more than a century, it has been the place where countries gathered in peace conferences and international courts to foster peace through justice.